Dear Hearts and Gentle People

A collection of entertaining tales

of

true life experiences

by

Heather Campbell

© Copyright 2004 Heather Campbell. All rights reserved.

No part of this publication may be reproduced, stored in a retrieval system, or transmitted, in any form or by any means, electronic, mechanical, photocopying, recording, or otherwise, without the written prior permission of the author.

Printed in Victoria, Canada

A cataloguing record for this book that includes the U.S. Library of Congress Classification number, the Library of Congress Call number and the Dewey Decimal cataloguing code is available from the National Library of Canada. The complete cataloguing record can be obtained from the National Library's online database at: www.nlc-bnc.ca/amicus/index-e.html
ISBN: 1-4120-3302-0

TRAFFORD

This book was published on-demand in cooperation with Trafford Publishing. On-demand publishing is a unique process and service of making a book available for retail sale to the public taking advantage of on-demand manufacturing and Internet marketing. **On-demand publishing** includes promotions, retail sales, manufacturing, order fulfilment, accounting and collecting royalties on behalf of the author.

Suite 6E, 2333 Government St., Victoria, B.C. V8T 4P4, CANADA
Phone   250-383-6864   Toll-free   1-888-232-4444 (Canada & US)
Fax   250-383-6804   E-mail   sales@trafford.com
Web site   www.trafford.com   TRAFFORD PUBLISHING IS A DIVISION OF TRAFFORD HOLDINGS LTD.
Trafford Catalogue #04-1129   www.trafford.com/robots/04-1129.html

10   9   8   7   6   5   4   3   2

I dedicate this book to all my friends and relatives who have encouraged me to write another book. Many of these people have been the subject matter for the stories in this book. They are truly *Dear Hearts and Gentle People*.

CONTENTS

Namely Us	8
More About Us	9

Marriage Moments

A Rose By Any Other Name	12
Absent Groom	14
Company Needed	17
No Exchange on P.J.'s	19
All in the Name of Love	20
Husband For Sale	23
The Nesting Instinct	25
Shades of Change	26

You Gotta Love Those Kids

Kindergarten Kids	30
A Child's View of the "Golden Years"	30
Cedar Lake Catastrophe	31
Great Reservations	33
Christmas Surprises	35

Family Snippets

Duplication in the Delivery Room	38
Flying Down the Trail	43
You Can't Escape the Long Arm of the Law	45
The Returned Prodigal	47
My Single Mother Adventure	49
The Power of Association	51
Aging and Me!	52
Campbells and the "Down Under"	55
Judging a Cookie By Its Cover	62
Tradition! Tradition!	63

Dear Hearts and Gentle People

A Night on the Town	68
Diane's Dilemma	69
Clap! Clap!	70
The Pregnant Grandmother	71
Do You Have Your Teeth?	74
Love Those "Newfies"	76
A Somewhat Smelly Tale	77
The Sun Doesn't Always Shine	79

Canine Tales

The Real Story of Chief	82
Dream Dog	83
Tale of Lorraine	86

Musically Inclined

Losing My Bite Over Elvis	90
Mr. Wallace's Surprise Symphony	92
A Special Gift	93
A Memorable Funeral	95

Bathroom Tales

Birthday Excitement	98
My "Locked Up" Experiences	99
The Interment	102

Life's Little Challenges

Looking Gift Horses in the Mouth	106
Hiding Your Skates in a Stump	107
Purse Packing Predicament	108
Cookie Stress	110
Whoa is Woe	112

Believe It or Not

Uncle Ab's Story	116
Getting to the Root of It	116
Campbell Duplication	119
"Paneless" Punctuality	121
Discipline Learned (or Not) in the Cadet Corps	122
Murphy's Law	124
The ABM Ate It	125
You Know You're Having a Bad Day When...	127
The "Origin" of Mother's Day, According to Frank	128

Acknowledgements

I am grateful to ever so many people who have helped me in the birthing of this book. Several have helped in the last few months of my manuscript preparation. Others have helped by their generous encouragement and advice through the years as I kept *pecking away* at my writing hobby.

Pecking away is an apt phrase to use when I say thanks to the talented members of the writing club here in Beachburg. We meet monthly and the name chosen for our group is "The Henscratchers". The critiquing and encouragement I have received from them has been so helpful. Not to be forgotten for the guidance I received when I was a member, is the Upper Valley Writers' Club, the former writing group to which I belonged.

In particular I thank my editor, Kathleen Burgess, for her thoroughness, her assistance and her helpful suggestions.

Once again, I am indebted to my husband Frank for all his technical support and his patience. For this book we also welcomed the technical assistance of our granddaughter, Amanda Gervais. We greatly appreciate her skills in the crafting of the title pages and the cover.

Finally, thank you friends and relatives for proofreading and giving consent for "your stories" to be published.

Dear Hearts and Gentle People

Namely Us

Many of the tales in this book are about events in the lives of Frank and myself, Heather. Few of you would have any way of knowing why our parents bestowed on us the names they did.

Frank was christened Francis Chester Campbell. Most of his buddies in his home area of Lake St.Peter and Maynooth, Ontario, know him only by his nickname "Chub" or "Chubby". At high school in Bancroft where I met him, the teachers called him by his given name of Francis. I followed along with this until I introduced him to Shirley Broslaw, the lady with whom I boarded in my first year of teaching at West Rouge. When she inquired later as to his whole name and I replied "Francis Chester Campbell", her eyebrows showed her disbelief as she asked, "Did his parents not like him?"

I had to laugh. I agreed it was a very daunting combination of names, but I knew he had been named after his grandfathers, Francis Campbell of Brighton, Ontario and Chester Card of Lake St.Peter.

After we were married and moved to a new location in 1964 and I realized that his engineering friends called him Frank, I adopted that too. At times having three different aliases causes confusion, but Frank has learned to answer to any of the three!

❦❦❦❦❦❦❦❦❦❦❦

My name of Heather Lorraine Gunter never caused any problems, but it could have been a different story. Before I was born my mother had the chosen name of "Gloria" selected if her baby was a girl. Thank goodness no name was put on any certificate at the Coe Hill Red Cross Hospital where I was born on Thanksgiving Sunday in 1940. Maybe it was an oversight, but I was sent home as "Baby Gunter". I am told that my Aunt Mary, Dad's sister who had no children of her own at that time, visited me every chance she got just to rock and cuddle me. When she learned that Mom and Dad planned to call me Gloria, she objected. This was so out of character for her, but she was adamant, saying, "Oh, you can't call her that! Can't you just hear the kids taunting "Here comes Glory Gunter!"

Thanks to Aunt Mary my name became Heather. What a relief! Little did anyone know at the time that I would one day marry a Campbell and end up with a name combination that causes people to think I must be truly Scottish.

More About Us

Frank and I had no idea that "our roots" would end up sharing common ground. Just this past summer he suggested that we visit the Grace Cemetery on the outskirts of Maynooth, on the road to Lake St.Peter. His purpose was to show me the gravestones of his grandfather, Chester Card, and his grandmother, Margaret Card. As we wandered around, imagine my disbelief when I found a tombstone marking the grave of my mother's grandfather, William Smith, and his wife, Blanche. They had lived in Lake St. Peter at one time, long before I was born. My memories of Great Grandpa Smith place him at Grandpa and Grandma Soble's in Ameliasburg, Ontario, when I would spend some summer holidays there as a child. His wife had already died and that is why he was living with his daughter Maria, my Grandma Soble. Great Grandpa Smith died when I was twelve and I had never inquired as to where he had been buried. I hope he doesn't mind that it has taken me this long to visit his grave and that it was really Chester Card who led me there. What a paradox life can be!

Dear Hearts and Gentle People

Author Heather at her Great Grandfather Smith's grave

Frank at his Grandfather Chester Card's grave

"Our Roots" in Grace Cemetery, near Maynooth, Ontario

Marriage Moments

A Rose By any Other Name ...

In the 1970's we moved to the small town of Beachburg, Ontario, not knowing a soul there. Frank's engineering firm, whose head office was in Peterborough, had a branch office in Pembroke. Frank had been sent to work out of the Pembroke office. After looking at several houses in the area, we chose one in Beachburg, just twenty minutes from Pembroke. We had no sooner settled in to our new location than Frank was sent back to Peterborough for several months of work. With two young children to care for, as well as my teaching job, I bravely tried to handle things at home through the week, knowing that Frank would be home on the weekend. It was not easy for either of us.

One Wednesday, upon opening the mail, I was startled to see a bill to Frank from the local florist for a dozen red roses. I knew for a fact that I had never received any roses! The date of purchase had been three weeks ago. Frank had never mentioned any such purchase to me, but his name and address were clearly at the top of the bill.

I had two full days to build up steam and imagine various scenarios. Frank had a Peterborough mistress, perhaps. But why would he buy flowers in Beachburg? Maybe they were wired to Peterborough. If not, then somebody here in Beachburg had received them. Did Frank already have another romantic interest here? Maybe there had been a mistake. I could phone the florist but how embarrassing it would be if I had to find out an unpleasant truth from the local florist. The old adage about the wife being the last to know burned in my mind.

By the time Friday night arrived, I was at the "I'll kill him" stage. How could he do this to me? The worst part was that I was afraid to talk to anyone about it. With no one to share, I had simmered and stewed alone. Frank had hardly made it through the door before I shoved the bill at him and demanded an explanation.

Frank was as puzzled as I. He could not explain. I could tell by the look on his face that this bill was a mystery. I felt a little sheepish and didn't confess all the dramas I had imagined.

The next morning Frank went to the florist shop. He explained the dilemma to Jean, the florist's sister, who worked in her brother's shop. Now it was Jean's turn to be embarrassed. She had sold the roses to Ron Lowe, another newcomer to Beachburg. He and Frank resembled each other so much and, with both men being relatively new to Beachburg, it had been an honest mistake. Jean had thought Ron was Frank and simply made out the bill that way. Ron's wife, Diane, received the roses and Frank's wife, Heather, received the bill!

Over the ensuing thirty years that we have lived in Beachburg, Frank and Ron have been mistaken for each other at various times, generally by people who didn't know either of them very well. None of the incidents have caused as much laughter, or has the story been told as many times, as has this story of the roses.

*Ron Lowe, Author Heather,
and Husband Frank*

The question: Which one sent the roses?

Absent Groom

Being abandoned at the altar is a nightmare that came true for an acquaintance of mine. Julie's wedding day was to be Saturday. Rehearsal was of course the Friday night before. The groom, Jeff, and his parents invited everyone back to their house for a rehearsal party buffet treat, the tradition in this area. Everyone was so happy and the cold salads, cold cuts, and cold drinks were a hit on such a warm evening. Most of the party left after an hour or two of mingling, but a few really close friends stayed until almost midnight. Jeff enjoyed their jokes and welcomed their support but knew that his parents were beginning to tire. With the last guest gone, Jeff insisted that Julie take his car and go too. After all, she was the bride and had a big day ahead. He'd help his parents clean up and then they'd all get some sleep.

Finally all the dishes were neatly stacked in the dishwasher and Jeff put the last leftover salad in the refrigerator. "Lights out!" he announced, "I'm exhausted."

Morning seemed to arrive too soon. The sunlight was blinding. Jeff staggered to his feet knowing that much was expected of him today. He started to pull on his sweat pants when suddenly he felt violently ill. He headed for the bathroom. The scene there wasn't pretty. A look in the mirror convinced him that he wasn't either. Just as he was emerging rather unsteadily from the bathroom, he heard his mom reminding him that she had bacon and eggs ready.

" I'm not hungry right now," he managed. Within seconds he was back in the bathroom.

"What is wrong with me? Is this what people call 'the wedding jitters'?" He felt weak, sweaty, and nauseous. It was now almost nine o'clock and the wedding was scheduled for three o'clock. Maybe he'd better call Julie.

"Jeff, I don't know," Julie sighed, "The emergency ward I think is the only answer. Have your dad take you. I'm in the midst of hair appointments for all of us, my fingernails have to be done, and there are still some last minute things to do at the church. I just cannot go with you." At that point it sounded to Jeff that Julie was crying.

Jeff managed a quick good-bye and headed for the bathroom for another round. Meanwhile, his father had already started the car and was waiting to take him to the hospital.

The emergency room was the usual plethora of people. Jeff did explain at the desk that he was being married at three o'clock. Even as he said it, he had his doubts. The ceremony would have to be fast- forwarded if it was to fit into the short span between his stomach cramps. While the minutes ticked by in the waiting room, he caught a look at his reflection mirrored in the nearby aquarium. Some groom he was going to make! The photographer's skills would never erase the grimace. The thought of having his picture taken right then ranked on a par with visits to his dentist.

Jeff noticed that even his father had started to pace the floor and check his watch. Maybe if they both broke out in a chorus of "Get Me to The Church On Time" it would speed things up!

They had waited well over an hour when finally Jeff's name was called. Once inside the examination room, Jeff described his symptoms, feeling sicker with each syllable.

"I can run some tests but from what you tell me I'm quite sure you are suffering from food poisoning," the doctor said.

"I had thought of that, but no one else from the party is sick. Why would I be the only one?"

" Did you eat anything while you were cleaning up?"

Jeff thought a minute. "Yes, I did eat two or three spoonfuls of a salad rather than stick such a little bit in the fridge."

"That could be your answer. It had likely been sitting too long and probably was an egg or maybe a fish mixture. Anyway, don't worry. By three o'clock this medicine that I am prescribing will have done its trick. You might still feel a little tired and empty but you'll be able to make the wedding."

Jeff checked his watch. It was almost noon. All he wanted to do right then was to lie down. He reminded his dad to call him by two o'clock, and headed for the bedroom as soon as they arrived home.

By half past two the guests, many who had come from far away, were assembling at the church, most of them unaware of any problem. Meanwhile Jeff, now accompanied by his best man, Kevin, was back at the hospital. Yes, he had managed to struggle into the rented tuxedo and looked like a groom on the outside, but his insides were writhing and he was so weak he could hardly navigate the corridor.

"You look like the most intoxicated groom I've ever seen," Kevin said.

"I almost wish I was. I'm sure I'd feel better than I do now."

The doctor still kept insisting he'd revive. "I'll keep you here in emergency to monitor you. Just tell the guests to come back in an hour. Make it a four o'clock wedding. What harm can there be?"

So, on the doctor's advice, Kevin telephoned the church, talked to both the minister and to Julie and they agreed to the hour's delay. Kevin promised to keep them posted and would keep his cell phone handy.

By four o'clock Jeff was much the same and by now Julie, splendid in her wedding gown, had been driven to the hospital.

At five o'clock the guests at the church were still waiting, thankful for the air-conditioning, and, of course, now fully aware of the problem. There was much milling around and visiting, but quietness descended when Jeff's father appeared in the pulpit.

"I have both good news and bad," he began. " At this moment the marriage vows are taking place between Jeff and Julie in a hospital room where Jeff has had to be admitted." He waited as the guests chorused their disappointment and concern. Then he continued. "The dinner set for six o'clock will still take place. The caterers are not a group that you can stall, and I am sure too that you will all want to eat by then. I'm not sure if the bride will be with us. I know the groom will not, but the rest of the family and wedding party will be there and the dance will follow the meal as planned."

This certainly was a wedding and a night to remember with an unequalled, unique chain of events. Julie did attend the meal, but for the rest of the evening she divided her time between the hospital room and the guests. The photographer was a real sport and edited the wedding video as quickly as he could so that just before the dance the video was shown. Jeff had been able to sit up in bed, the wedding party had all been in attendance, and the minister was able to convey a reverent and meaningful ambiance to the whole ceremony.

I'm sure it was not the wedding, nor the wedding night, that Jeff and Julie had even in their wildest dreams anticipated, but it was one nobody would ever forget. I'm happy to report that Jeff did recover in a few days and a much-appreciated honeymoon did take place, but it was years before Jeff could truly enjoy salads again!

Company Needed

Some people are proudly independent and able to live alone while others are not. I like to think I am independent, but experience has proven that I might not be able to live by myself. I had a taste of it when I was a new bride. Frank worked away from home all week. Daytime for me was not a problem because I was teaching school. Nighttime was a different story. Each evening I came home to a lonely apartment in an urban setting where not even the person next door knew my name. Even my landlord, living in the same building, was only a friend on the day I was handing him the monthly rent cheque.

Quite often I invited Connie, the ten-year old who had been the flower girl at our wedding, to come and have supper and spend the night.

I don't think my problem was the fear of being alone. There were other people in the building and I figured I could scream loudly if the situation demanded it.

I do think I had a problem with loneliness. When Connie wasn't there, I usually ate my meals in front of the television while I watched "The Perry Como Show". I was actually seeing more of Perry than I was of Frank.

Things went along not too badly until one evening I became ill. I was nauseated and had a great deal of stomach pain. I went to bed hoping that I could fall asleep. I didn't. The pain seemed to become worse. I spent several hours groaning, moaning and crying, interspersed with trips to the bathroom. Then I began having trouble breathing and became dizzy, sweaty, and felt too weak to even get to the bathroom. I crawled to the phone and called Connie's mother in the middle of the night. My mouth was so dry I had difficulty forming my words and I know I scared her with my tale.

"Heather," she said, "I'm going to call the fire department. They're right across the road from you. They'll be able to help. Maybe you'll have to go to the hospital."

I was too weak to argue. I actually wondered if I was dying.

Two burly firemen equipped with a stretcher arrived within minutes. Through my tears I managed to tell them my troubles. I was rather startled to notice that one of them was making a pouch of an ordinary brown paper bag.

"Blow into this bag," he said holding it to my mouth and nose. "Keep exhaling and inhaling. I'll hold it for you until you feel able." And he did, encouraging me with each puff. Finally I felt myself regaining strength and I relaxed a little.

"Good, " he said. "You're looking better," and he took the bag away.

"What do you think is wrong with me?"

"You are here alone, aren't you, and you have been doing a lot of crying and maybe moaning?" he asked.

"Yes, I have had pains in my stomach."

"Well, I think you are right now suffering from hyperventilation. That happens when we breathe out too much carbon dioxide. If this ever happens again, just get a bag and do what we've done here now. We'll still take you to the hospital to have you checked out but I suspect they might say you are suffering from high anxiety."

A ride in the fire truck and a check of my vital signs proved the fireman correct. The kind doctor's advice was, "I don't think you should be living alone."

Since then I've had great admiration for people who contentedly live by themselves, and a great deal of empathy for any of these people who have the misfortune of becoming ill.

No Exchange on P.J.'s

Heather Campbell

"Darn, after all my careful shopping and painstaking price-comparison, they don't fit," I said to the mirror, viewing myself with disdain. "It's pretty embarrassing when even pyjamas are too tight!"

Maybe joining the weight-watching group wouldn't be such a bad idea, I mused as I folded up the p.j.'s and stuffed them back in the store's shopping bag along with the receipt.

Oh well, I thought, since I have to drive back to town early in the morning for my dentist appointment, I'll return them then. Maybe I'll look for a more accommodating style. Buying a size bigger than large would be an absolute last alternative, even for pyjamas!

I sat the bag on the cupboard, but then remembering how absent-minded I had been lately, I decided I'd better hang the bag right on the doorknob where I could not possibly miss it as I headed out. Mornings were definitely not my best times.

It wasn't until I was in the dentist chair the next day and had nothing better to do than collect my thoughts, that I reflected on the pyjamas in a bag hanging on the doorknob. Why had I not noticed the bag there when I went out this morning? Now here I was, a half hour from home and where was that bag? Every so often, between my "uh-haw's" to the dentist and my frowns directed to his assistant who kept forcing more and more into my mouth, I replayed the pyjama mystery. What had happened to them? Was I sleepwalking this morning when I left and totally missed seeing the bag?

That evening at home over supper, I mentioned my dilemma to my better-half. At first there was no comment, but then he asked, "Was it a yellow bag?"

"Yes!" I brightened, realizing that he must have seen it.

"This was garbage morning, wasn't it?" he asked, forming his question slowly, almost as if he was afraid of the answer.

"Yes, you always put the garbage out on Tuesdays," I replied, at first wondering what that had to do with the pyjamas. Then I made the connection!

"You put that bag in the garbage, didn't you?"

"Yes, I figured that's why you had hung it at the door. I guessed that you had not wanted to go out in the cold. I never even looked in the bag to see what it was. I'm not in the habit of inspecting the garbage."

Well, what could I say? It was an honest mistake. Accidents happen, as my granddaughter is always quick to remind me.

Another favourite expression of hers, "Behind every cloud is a silver lining" played itself out too a few months later. When I opened the Christmas gift from my husband, there lay the most beautiful pair of pyjamas that I have ever had in my life. Thank goodness they were a perfect fit.

All in the Name of Love

Our friends are sometimes the subjects of our best stories. Unfortunately our friend Hilda is no longer with us, but many years ago she told me this story about one summer in the early years of her marriage.

Picton Airport was built in the summer of 1940. Hilda's husband Frank had a dump truck and he was able to get work there. He tried boarding for the first week of the job but, when he came home to Hilda in Ormsby that week-end, he said that he didn't like the landlady's meals and that Hilda would have to come back with him. That meant that toddler Terry and baby Donna would also be coming.

Although love was abundant for these two in their early years of marriage, money wasn't, so Frank borrowed two tents. They packed their gas stove, some dishes and some bedding. They also took their couch that opened up into a bed and the mattress from the big crib. Frank placed some boards on the ground beside the bed and the large mattress went on those to make a bed for Terry. At the foot of their bed, they set up a smaller crib for Donna. One tent was the bedroom and the other was the kitchen, complete with gas stove, table, and some folding chairs. These tents were set up in a kind farmer's yard whose property would eventually be taken over by the airport. The elderly farmer and his wife still lived in the farmhouse but would inevitably have to move.

The days were long for Hilda and the two children. Frank left for work at 6 o'clock in the morning and didn't return until 6:30 in the evening.

About two weeks into their stay, there was a terrible thunderstorm with torrential rains and fierce wind. The bedroom tent leaked, but somehow the family managed to get to sleep. Suddenly they were awakened by a gush of water and gales of wind. The storm had pulled the stakes out of the side of the tent and the wind was carrying the rain into the tent with great force. Hilda jumped up and grabbed Terry at the same time as Frank was bundling up Donna. There was no time to look for coats. They ran as best they could against the storm towards the farmhouse, with the children in their arms, trying to keep them sheltered. Frank repeatedly pounded on the door. With the noise of the storm it took a long time before the old couple finally heard them. The old man, wearing only a short nightgown, appeared at the door. As soon as he realized who it was and the plight they were in, he was anxious to help.

"You can sleep in my bed," he said. "I'll go upstairs with my wife." He ushered them into his bedroom and Hilda noticed immediately that the bed had no sheets, just army blankets.

Because Hilda's nightgown and the babies' blankets were soaking wet, Frank went back through the storm to get the suitcases and his work clothes. When he returned, his clothes that had become wet in the tent had to be put over chair backs to dry so he'd be able to go to work. Hilda changed both herself and Terry and Donna into dry clothes from the suitcases and they all snuggled into bed. The kids went to sleep but Hilda and Frank, although glad to be safe and dry, found the army blankets pretty uncomfortable and didn't sleep much in spite of their exhaustion.

While Frank was at work the next day, Hilda had the job of pinning all the wet garments and bedding to the clothesline. She took down the damaged, wet tent and let the sun get at the mattresses to dry them out. She decided the kitchen didn't really need a tent if the weather co-operated so she took down that tent and moved it to accommodate the dry mattresses. Then she made up the beds.

Supper was ready when Frank got back from work. Everyone being exhausted, they ate and immediately went to bed, glad to be back in their own cozy sheets.

Hilda was awakened early the next morning by Donna's whimpering. She listened but didn't move, hoping Donna would go back to sleep. Then she heard vomiting followed by more whimpering. She sprang out of bed to find Donna in a mess. A downpour of rain might have been a welcome thing at this point! With no bath or shower available, Hilda cleaned her up as best she could and cuddled her in bed until morning.

Frank had to leave for work, but Donna was still really sick. Because Donna had had stomach upsets before, Hilda knew the doctor advised no food and only barley water to drink for two days. After that, milk was to be introduced gradually. Hilda did the best she could until Frank came home. Then they headed for Grandpa and Grandma Tice's in Belleville. Thank goodness for grandparents!

Hilda and the kids stayed in Belleville for almost a week. By then Donna was better. Grandpa was reluctant to have his daughter and grandchildren return to a tent, so he drove them back to Picton to look at a house that Frank had mentioned was near the airport and possibly for rent. It took some time to find the owner and make the arrangements and then on the way back to the tent they became lost. It was pitch-black dark when they reached the tent, but with the help of the headlights on Grandpa's car, they took the tent down, loaded everything in the truck, and by midnight were back at the house.

It was a treat to be in a house rather than a tent, but this house had no stove or furnace. It was one of the coldest summers on record. There were days that Hilda cleaned up the breakfast, dressed the kids in the warmest clothes they had, and hiked over to the edge of the airport. When Frank came by with the dump truck, they all climbed in and rode around with him, just to keep warm until noon. Then off they went home so the kids could have their lunch and their afternoon naps under some warm blankets. Hilda meanwhile was dressed in layers of sweaters while she prepared supper.

Another Ormsby friend, Mac Park, eventually came to work at the airport, and he asked to stay with Hilda and Frank, in spite of the house having no heat. The fact that there was no bed was not a problem. The pioneer spirit was an undaunted one. Mac took the tents and folded them in such a way as to make a bed in one of the upstairs rooms. He was glad of the company and the good meals, and Hilda and Frank appreciated his help with the rent. If Hilda had stayed longer than that summer, I'm sure she would have been operating one of the first "bed and breakfast" establishments. As it was, I think she was glad to see the end of that summer and get back to the true comforts of home in little Ormsby.

Husband for Sale

> **HUSBAND FOR SALE**
> Comes with computer!

These words are printed on a sign that has been hanging near our front door for over a year. A few weeks ago I was thinking of having it printed in the classified section of our newspaper!

To understand why, you first have to know our set-up. We have three computers: mine, his, and a laptop which is also his. Husband is quite gifted in, and addicted to, computers, and spends more time each week with his computer than he does with me. That was the reason for the sign, given by an understanding friend at Christmas time.

Husband works out of town all week and is home on weekends only. He takes his laptop with him for business purposes. We both share the same e-mail address. On Sunday night I e-mailed a writing buddy. It was about an upcoming reading she and I were to be part of and I needed some more information. I always e-mail her because telephoning is a long distance charge. I waited a full two days, checking morning, noon and evening for her reply. Then I repeated the same message and sent it again. Another two days passed and still there had been no reply.

I was getting worried. I had to have the answer by Thursday night at the latest because the reading was on Friday. Long distance costs were no longer a factor. I telephoned. I listened to the repeated ringing and hoped that an answering machine would pick up. That didn't happen. Now what? It was a thirty-minute drive and, even if I was that foolish, what guarantee did I have that she was at home? I certainly was not suffering from writers' block. I imagined all sorts of scenarios that could have happened!

When Husband came home a day earlier than planned, I told him of my dilemma, not that I figured he could do anything about it, but it's therapeutic to blow off steam.

" What is your friend's name?" he asked.

I told him and wondered why he wanted to know.

" I think I saw a name like that when I was pulling in some business e-mail this week. I'll check," he said as he headed to his home office in our basement.

Well, what a learning experience for me! That was the first time that I knew that he ever had to use the e-mail for his business. I had seen only drafting and plotting squiggles any time that I had passed his screen. I am not a tech-wizard and so until this epiphany, I had no idea that his pulling in the e-mails on either of his computers meant that I would never see them on my screen. That means if Husband pulls in my e-mail, he has to either print out a hard copy and give it to me or remember to verbally give me the message. A snail-mail comparison for any of you who are not computer literate would be someone going to the post office with your key, getting your mail, and never telling you.

Needless to say, when Husband returned from the basement he had in his hand not one, but two letters from my buddy. My questions had dutifully been answered in these letters. At last I had all the information I needed and I knew there was a God! I was still a little testy that I had gone through all that anxiety simply because my mail had been intercepted by a less-than-reliable mailman, but, to quote Shakespeare, "All's well that ends well."

Nevertheless, the *Husband For Sale* sign remains. Just maybe someday I'll get an offer too good to resist!

Heather Campbell

The Nesting Instinct

Friend Neil says rather unhappily that he knows it's really spring when wife Janet gets the "nesting instinct ". I think I'm beginning to understand what he means because I seem to have a renovating obsession this year, which in the bird world must be akin to building my nest. Each day my compulsions grow stronger and my list grows longer.

Already I have bought a new bedspread and dust ruffle and have great plans for making matching drapes. The wallpaper simply must be stripped, the ceiling painted, and a colour chosen for the walls that will match the bedspread. The bedroom carpet is thirty years old and should be replaced, but any mention of that makes the male bird at our house fly around at a very strange angle. Maybe the carpet will have to be part of next year's nest.

The windows all need cleaning and that means I'll wash all the curtains and have the drapes cleaned too. If I'm going to do all that, I might as well book the carpet cleaners. While they are here, they can shampoo the chesterfield suite too.

The yard is a disgrace and must be raked. That means the rakes come out of the shed and the winter shovels go in. Taking down outdoor Christmas decorations and finding them a home should have been done yesterday. But how can a person be outside when so many jobs need to be done inside?

I spend an entire afternoon pulling everything out of the linen closet, wiping the shelves, and putting the linens back. It is astounding what I discover in that closet! Certainly more than linens have found a home in there. I retrieve hair bows that no one had had in their hair for years, outdated hair rollers, and that long lost traveling iron. Will I remember that I've stored it this time in the otherwise empty black suitcase? It seemed a logical place at the time.

The cleaning of the kitchen cupboards is next on my list, just as soon as my granddaughter can come and help. I've convinced myself it's a two-person job. Any mention of the male bird helping and he begins that strange flight pattern again.

The winter boots were put away in good faith last week.

This is to be followed by the cleaning and laundering of all winter coats, scarves, hats and mitts, and then away to the cedar closet they go. But that means the spring and summer coats must come out. Along with that is my own personal wardrobe that has been in a bit of a transitional mode these last few weeks of uncertain weather. Now I think it's time to make a permanent change. Male bird's closet is much easier. In the winter he wears clothes from the left side. In the summer he switches to the right side. Somehow I seem to require more plumage than one closet will hold!

In fact, I could use more shelves in every room. I need to get those towering piles of books and magazines off the floor.

Will I hire a carpenter or risk counting on male bird to do it? Right now the male bird is studying me intently and thinks perhaps I am getting carried away with this nest.

Would he be happier with the drab-looking cowbird that seems perfectly content to never build a nest? It just lays its eggs in another bird's nest and lets them take care of it all.

I'm sure there will come a day when I'll welcome that arrangement. In the meantime, I'll keep the carpenter's number handy!

Shades of Change

After forty years of marriage why do I expect that my chosen one is going to change? He hates change, change of any kind! I'm sure he'd be perfectly happy if we were still living in our first apartment with one bedroom and a living room so small that you could almost put your feet in the kitchen sink when you sat on the chesterfield.

We have lived in our present house for almost thirty years. We were the first owners. In the beginning each room that we painted or papered was fun, as we made this our home rather than living with the builder's choice of décor. Occasionally over the years, we've had minor changes such as a closet added or a room repainted. As long as the change wasn't too radical and I didn't ask my chosen one to do it, our matrimonial boat bobbed along with only a ripple now and then.

One of these ripples occurred when I acquired a whole new set of cupboards and a new layout in the kitchen. This was quite a challenge for my captain. When wanting a knife or fork, he repeatedly went to the drawer that originally had the cutlery, opened it, saw the array of cooking utensils, closed it as quietly as possible and did a neat forty-five degree pivot to the correct drawer. This went on for months as I stifled my giggles and pretended not to notice. It was much the same thing when he wanted a cup. Finally he started carrying his cup-of-the-day with him and that solved the cup problem for that day anyway.

This spring I decided I could not stand the wallpaper in our bedroom any longer. After twenty years, a change was long overdue. I wanted the walls painted. "Hire it done," he said. And so I did. I went all out and changed the colour scheme from rose tones to soft yellow. That meant that nothing in the way of spread, curtain or blind could be reused. The painter worked long hours on stripping the stubborn wallpaper and then painted the new colour that matched the new bedspread and carpet. It sure did look wonderful! I paid the painter who is also a carpenter and who offered to do any other little jobs. I said we'd take care of the window treatment because I wasn't sure what I wanted.

That was a mistake. I finally decided on the new Roman-type shades, the ones with the tiny bamboo slats. They come with their own hardware and directions that say "easy installation". I was really anxious to see the room finished so I asked "my captain" to do the installing.

"Does it have to be tonight?" he asked.

"We really don't have any other free nights this week," I reminded him.

So he began. Out of the box came the Roman shade and the hardware with directions in such tiny print that you scarcely could read it without a magnifying glass. I was sent for the ladder and the drill.

"Was the old blind broken?" he asked when I returned.

"No."

"So why aren't we just putting it back up?"

"Because it's pink!" I declared.

"Humph," he snorted.

Finally with much sighing and an occasional witnessing,

the first bracket was installed on the window casing.

"That's never going to hold this shade," he announced.

"Why not?"

"Because that shade weighs at least fifty pounds," he exclaimed rather loudly.

I thought it best not to contradict, but I had carried that shade, box and all, from the Sears store to the van and then from the van to the house. To me it felt little heavier than perhaps two ten pound bags of potatoes. But over the years I had learned it's not wise to argue with the captain.

As we stood there weighing the situation, the phone rang. Did we know that our dog was loose? Would we come and get him? More snarling ensued, but not from the dog. Judging by the slam of the door, our poor dog would be the recipient of more witnessing.

It looked like I might have to call in the Romans for sure to deal with this shade.

With the dog now ushered back into the house, the irritation level seemed even higher.

"I'll put it up but it will all come crashing down! You just wait! I don't see why you wanted anything this fancy. Why wouldn't an ordinary blind do?"

I hate to think where this all might have ended had not our daughter happened to pick that hour to come to use our computer. Things were tense until she said, "Here Dad. I'll give you a hand with that." I took that as my cue to leave. A nice warm bath in the whirlpool tub with the jets turned high enough that I couldn't hear any other sounds was definitely the order of the evening.

When I emerged fully relaxed twenty minutes later, the Roman shade was in place and looked admirable.

The captain was watching T.V. and waiting for my approval of his handiwork. The sea was calm.

I think I'll enjoy drifting along for awhile before I tell him that I'll need new hardware installed above the shade for draping the swag that I plan to purchase!

You Gotta Love Those Kids

Some of the stories that follow talk about our children, Laurie and Kevin, who are now adults and will probably someday tell their own stories. In other tales you will find mention of our granddaughters, Amanda and Jessica, now both in their teens. Still others relate endearing facts about friends, relatives, or acquaintances. All those concerned have given permission for the sharing of these memoirs.

Kindergarten Horror

Daughter Laurie, now in her thirties, just recently told me about her experience at five years of age when we lived in Whitby. I guess she was too uncertain of the truth at the time of this happening to share it with me.

Laurie's kindergarten teacher, Miss Knapp, was a delight and the whole class worshipped her. But children being children, Miss Knapp often had cause to say, "You're turning my hair gray" or "Now I know why my hair is turning gray."

Laurie says she will never forget the day that Miss Knapp entered the classroom and her hair was completely gray. She said a hush fell over the room and each child stared in disbelief. In her own mind Laurie remembers thinking, "We have been really bad and Miss Knapp, the teacher that I love, has now had all her hair turn gray just like she warned us was going to happen." Laurie thinks she was just about to break into tears when Miss Knapp said with a little grin, " Did I fool you?" and then reached up and pulled off the gray wig! Much to the children's relief, Miss Knapp's beautiful brown hair was still there.

A Child's View of the Golden Years

As people reach those "golden years" they look forward to freedom and a taste of luxury. Retired Ontario friends of ours have lived the winter months for the past few years in a large RV park in Arizona. This RV park, like most, is a whole community of recreational vehicles, each occupying a tiny rented lot just big enough to accommodate the vehicle and within spitting distance of the neighbouring vehicle on either side. Annual membership fees entitle the occupants to planned activities and entertainment all within the confines of the park. Our friends told us this story about a little girl who came to the trailer park to visit her grandparents. When she returned home, her teacher asked her to write a story about her holiday. Her story went something like this:

"My grandpa and grandma live in this fenced-in place where everyone lives in tin boxes. Everyone there is retarded and they must be very forgetful because they all have to wear their nametags on their chests. There is also a guard at the gate to make sure that none of them get outside the fence by themselves."

Just like beauty is in the eye of the beholder, it seems the same applies to the concept of how to enjoy life.

Cedar Lake Catastrophes

It was June and the Parkside teaching staff and our families had been invited by one of the staff members to her cottage for a year-end celebration. Although we had never been to this lake or cottage before, the map was explicit. Laurie, our three-year old and only child at the time, was excited and kept expecting each cottage along the road to be the one. "I bet it's the next one, Daddy," she said, each time we passed a cottage. Finally after slowing down at ever so many driveways, we spotted the sign "The Cedars". We had arrived.

The cottage was on a bit of a knoll and in front stretched a beach and a long wooden dock. Some of the staff were indoors, others were setting up lawn chairs outside the cottage and a few were already in swimming. Husband Frank knew very few so I tried to introduce both him and Laurie amid the bustle of unpacking trunks and coolers. We had all brought food and drinks.

"I hope you brought your suit, " Pat the hostess said. "The swimming is great but be careful of the drop-off from the dock. It's wonderful for docking boats but is about six feet deep."

I assured her that both Laurie and I had our suits but not Frank. In fact, Laurie was ready so I'd better soon get my suit on.

Of course we all loved to visit too. We taught together but we did not get much time to really know one another and their families. This was a wonderful chance to do that. Finally Laurie and I did make our way to the beach and she enjoyed both the water and the sand and joined a few other children in making a sandcastle.

I wandered over to some fellow staff members sitting in chairs on the beach. We passed the time chatting and sharing munchies as our children played.

Suddenly I was aware that a man was running from near the cottage, throwing lawn chairs out of his way, and coming full tilt down the slope to the beach. On second look I realized it was Frank! What was wrong with him? Was he angry? Was he drunk?

He headed straight to the dock, ran the length of it and jumped off fully clothed, disappearing into the depths of water there. We all watched speechless. I felt scared and suddenly nauseated. I had not even thought of Laurie until suddenly she appeared in the water where her Dad had jumped in. He was pushing her up on the dock and they both were sputtering and coughing, but then she began giggling. It was then that I realized that Frank had seen Laurie from where he had been standing while I, obviously, had just taken for granted that she was still playing with the group.

I ran to her and wrapped her in a towel while other people gave Frank a hand up onto the dock. "What happened? I didn't see her jump in."

"She didn't jump. She just let herself off the side of the dock ever so slowly and disappeared!"

Now I really was sick. How could I have let her out of my sight? She was still giggling but shivering too. Someone suggested that we go to the barbecues and she would feel warmer there. Frank, meanwhile, went to the cottage to put on some dry clothes that our host was lending him.

Feeling like the worst mother of the year, I hugged her to me and carried her to a lawn chair near one of the barbecues. Most of the food from coolers had been put on the picnic tables by now and so after a little cuddling, I left Laurie in the chair and went to get her some food. I returned just in time to see the second disaster.

Laurie was bent over forward, pulling her lawn chair closer to the fire. With her head down, her long brown hair was inching closer to the fire, and yes, her hair was on fire! Now I was the one running! I got to her as fast as I could and began slapping the top of her head, much to Laurie's surprise. "Your hair is on fire, Honey! What were you trying to do?"

"I just wanted to get warmer, Mommy," she whimpered.

By now I had the burning hair smothered and only the putrid smell remained. "I think we'll be taking the scissors to this when we get home. What a day this has been!"

It was a party I would never forget, but I was glad that I could identify with Shakespeare's " All's Well That Ends Well ".

Great Reservations

Each summer for the last few years it has been a treat to take our granddaughters on a long-weekend trip to some place of interest in Ontario. Some years we are more prepared than others.

On one of these not-so-well-prepared summers as we were frantically stuffing last minute things into our van in anticipation of departing as soon as possible, I had a rational moment.

"Maybe I should make a reservation. Where do you think we'll be by bedtime tonight, Grandpa?" I asked my husband.

"Oh let's just play it by ear and pull in whenever we are tired."

I had learned many years ago not to argue with his wisdom, especially if it looked like any discussion would delay us. In his eyes, the best kind of trip would be one where you took only a toothbrush and a change of underwear and you had no definite plans. The packing and unpacking of luggage is too time-consuming for his gypsy nature. So we left mid-afternoon, destination uncertain.

About 200 miles this side of Niagara Falls the kids started pointing out motels that had vacancy signs.

"Look Grandma, that motel looks nice."

"But it's only 8:00 P.M., much too early. We'll drive for another half hour anyway," Grandpa said.

"Oh look over there, Grandpa. It's almost 8:30 and that one looks good."

"The traffic is too heavy for me to cross to that side of the road. Watch for something on this side."

Finally about 9:00 P.M., we pulled into a motel on the right side of the road. As usual, I was sent in to book a room.

"I'm sorry, Madam, we have been full for the last hour."

" Well, no problem," Grandpa says," We have several hotel card-memberships. We'll phone and have them book their nearest available hotel or motel."

Much to our dismay, each call produced the same reply. "There is nothing available in a 60 mile radius."

Apparently there were several conventions that weekend and every nearby room was full. We were forced to drive for another hour, finally ending up in Niagara Falls where we were able to get the last room available at an Econo-Lodge. It was right on the river and cost a mere $249.00 for *one* night!!! Our granddaughters, who at that time had seldom stayed at motels, thought it was the most beautiful room in the world. Grandpa and Grandma thought it was pretty ordinary but were glad to have a place to finally rest their heads.

By the time we were booked into our rooms it was 11:00 P.M. and the view of the river that I guess we must have been paying for was something that maybe we'd try and appreciate in the morning. When we thought of all those motels with vacancy signs that we had passed three hours ago, we did agree with our granddaughters' advice, "You should have listened to the kids."

Needless to say, a damper was put on Grandpa's gypsy spirit. I hear far less static from him now when I insist on booking a room for at least the first night of any trip we plan.

Granddaughters Amanda and Jessica Gervais
1995

Christmas Surprises

Friend Leanne prides herself on organization, especially at Christmas. This year was no exception. The tree was resplendent with decorations. The traditional Christmas village was set up in the entranceway. Poinsettia and holly trimmed the mantle. Lights twinkled everywhere. The shopping was finished. As soon as Leanne had all the Christmas gifts beautifully wrapped and labeled, she placed them under the tree to complete the holiday setting.

She and Wayne had a dinner engagement that night but hired a babysitter for Corey and Melissa who were ages eight and nine. They left knowing that everything was ready for Christmas a week early. Now they could relax and enjoy pre-Christmas celebrations.

It was late when they returned. Leanne turned off the Christmas lights quickly and checked on the children who were sleeping soundly. Everyone enjoyed a peaceful night.

The next morning as Leanne sat down in front of the tree with her second cup of coffee, she admired the trimmings from top to bottom. It was when her gaze reached the bottom, that she noticed a flaw. One of the gifts seemed to be coming unwrapped on one corner. She set her coffee aside and had a closer look. Not just one, but several gifts were bulging and no longer had the neatly folded corners that she had made when she wrapped them. Each of these gifts was addressed to Melissa!

Wayne had taken this cherub and her brother to the arena so Leanne was alone. She thought of different tactics she could use. Although she felt a little disappointed, she decided not to accuse.

Later that day she casually asked Melissa what she was hoping she would receive for Christmas. Melissa stammered a little but then began naming exactly the things that were in those bulging gifts. Leanne was tempted to let this deceit scenario continue and see if Melissa could act surprised as she opened the gifts. Then she reconsidered and decided that it was time to point out to Melissa the fun she would be missing on Christmas morning.

A few tears were shed but no more scolding was done. After all, experience is the best teacher. However, just to show who is in control at this house, the next year the gifts were sitting under the tree a week early, but this time instead of names, the gifts were numbered, and only Leanne knew the secret code!

Family Snippets

Duplication in the Delivery Room

For my second child, I was admitted to the maternity ward just at suppertime. The examining doctor told us there was still plenty of time before the baby would arrive and so, at my insistence, husband Frank left the hospital to get himself something to eat.

An hour later as he stepped from the elevator, he heard a passing nurse say to another, "Heather Campbell just had a baby boy."

Surprised that the baby had arrived already, but thrilled that our daughter now had a baby brother, Frank headed for the delivery room. Luckily, I recognized his coat as he sped past the labour room door where I was still battling it out. It gave me great satisfaction at that point to scream out his name! In a few seconds he appeared in the doorway, his face etched with worry and puzzlement.

"The nurse said that Heather Campbell had just had a baby boy. What's going on? Is everything O.K.?"

In the hour that he had been gone, I had learned an interesting, almost unbelievable fact. Little did I realize the entanglements that lay ahead.

"There is another Heather Campbell here," I explained. "She was admitted shortly before I was!"

We didn't have much time to speculate on what the odds were of this happening because just then I started having stronger, relentless contractions. Within forty minutes the same report was made again – "Heather Campbell just had a baby boy."

When I was finally wheeled into the recovery room, the nurse said, "Heather Campbell, I'd like you to meet Heather Campbell." The other Heather was waiting to be taken to her own room. We laughed about the uniqueness of our situation and discovered that, not only had we each had a baby boy, but that their weights differed by only one ounce!

Hours later as I lay alone in my room trying to rest, I was disturbed even further by the conversation of nurses in the hallway. My attention was really alerted when I overheard "...and they have the nerve to have the same first names too!" These words planted in my mind the first seeds of doubt, seeds that were given much nurturing in the next few days.

Even by the next morning, these doubts had sprouted to the extent that when our baby, who we now called Kevin, was brought to me for his first feeding, I looked into his tiny, red face and thought, "He looks so different than he did last night."

That evening when Frank and his mother came to visit, the nurse at the desk sent then to the wrong nursery. They stood, faces pressed to the glass, admiring the other Campbell baby until the mistake was discovered. I sensed an inner panic when they related this to me but, for their sake, I tried to laugh it off and remain calm on the outside.

On the second day, the nursery attendant pointed out that Kevin now had an identification bracelet on each ankle, one saying Campbell and the other having our doctor's name. She explained that when duplication of surnames appeared, the usual procedure was to put the mother's first name on the second bracelet. In our extraordinary case however, this would not have clarified anything. Thank goodness we both did not have the same doctor! As I thanked her for her concern and explanation, I could not suppress the thought that perhaps the mistake had already been made the night of the births. I was sure I had read of such hospital errors having happened elsewhere.

This was in the 60's when the mother and baby had a week's hospital stay. Sometime later during that week I noticed with horror that, although the correct doctor's name was on Kevin's ankle, the name of the other Campbell baby's doctor was on his basket. How could this have occurred and what did this suggest?

I also learned that earlier in our confinement my admittance record had been taken to the other Heather for some updating. She recognized the mistake when she noticed her age listed as 28. Any woman does a double-check when she is suddenly regarded as ten years older!

Roses sent to me by Frank were delivered in the same manner with the nurse announcing, "Flowers from your hubby!" Heather told me that she sat admiring them for a good ten minutes before she noticed the attached card saying "Love Frank". Her husband's name is Pete.

That same day a nurse woke me saying, "Your mother is here to see you. Come on in, Mrs. Stewart." Confusion reigned again. I did not even know a Mrs. Stewart. Who was this woman? Well, you guessed it! She belonged to the other Heather Campbell. Frank and I had unknowingly compounded the complexity of the duplication by naming or son "Kevin Stewart". The nurse had naturally thought that a Mrs. Stewart would have to be Kevin Stewart's grandmother. Instead she really belonged with "Pete Junior". And so the plot thickened.

During the remaining, stressful three days, our meals, mail, and ministers, all reached wrong destinations and had to be re-routed. By then I think we two Heathers had both decided that we should be sharing a room so we could quickly sort out the blunders. That didn't happen,

After my discharge from the hospital, my doubts still continued to grow. Kevin did not in the least resemble his sister, nor did he seem to resemble anyone in the family. Friends often commented on this, not realizing the mental torture they were causing me. Rather than give voice to my fears I would usually reply, "Oh, I think it's because he is so bald. He'll look different when he grows some hair."

Then one day my mother-in-law said to me, "You know, I think that you have the wrong baby!" That did it! I had to know the truth now. I couldn't go on like this. I wanted my own child. Did I have him or not?

I immediately made an appointment with our doctor. I said it was an emergency and told his receptionist that she'd have to trust me because I couldn't share the details with her. I had never even totally shared them with Frank.

Up to that point, because I had had an obstetrician attending me, our doctor had not been fully aware of my hospital experiences. I was pleased however, to learn that he did know all the facts about Kevin. Obstetricians, I was told, leave the care of the baby to the family doctor.

He listened quietly as I poured out my story. Then he shook his head. "You should have come to me sooner," he admonished. "You've risked being a schizophrenic-mother, afraid to give a total love-commitment to this baby for fear he is not yours."

Sitting down across from me, he handed me a tissue to help stop my tears, and in a kind, fatherly way assured me that all the details of Kevin's birth records had been carefully checked and there was no doubt that he belonged to us. He did not laugh at me as I had dreaded, but told me that he certainly understood. It is natural to want your own flesh and blood. Then he gave me an order.

"Now that I have put your mind at rest, I never want to hear you even suggest these doubts again. Put them entirely out of your mind and enjoy your son!"

That is just what we have been doing now for close to 35 years. Today that little red-faced baby, who initially didn't seem to resemble any of us, looks so much like me and acts and sounds so much like Frank that any one would wonder how I ever could have doubted his identity!

(If I had not kept a journal, I would not have been so accurate with details after this long time.)

*Laurie and Kevin
Early 1970's*

*Would hair
have made him
look more like
his sister?*

In Grandma Campbell's farm kitchen

Heather Campbell

Flying Down The Trail

Our son Kevin came into the world with a rush, four days earlier than expected, and he's been rushing ever since.

He has always loved anything with a motor and wheels. As a toddler, his favourite toys were trucks and cars. Then once he was old enough to be introduced to saws and metal cutters, we often found he had remodeled his toys. Two vehicles often became one. And so it continued until he was old enough to have his first motor-powered "toy". For his sixteenth birthday we bought him a Motocross bike. The only stipulations that we made were that he must always wear a helmet and he was to do his riding on a vacant, rather isolated piece of land known as "the springs".

A couple of friends had motorbikes and it became a regular thing for them to meet at "the springs" which was only about two miles away from our house. Besides being spacious, the terrain there lent itself to some "Evel Knieval" style riding. We never heard any bad reports and satisfied ourselves that these young lads were having a good time, and at least they were not bothering neighbours with their noise.

After a few months though, Wally, who owned a small plane and was the father of Karl, one of Kevin's friends, saw Frank down town and flagged him down.

"I just want to let you know that I am not happy about you buying Kevin that bike," he said.

"Why is that, Wally?"

"Well, because now Karl wants one and they're not safe."

"Why do you say that?"

"Because your son Kevin is riding at break-neck speeds on the old ski-doo trail from the Gun Club to "the springs". He's going to kill himself. A sixteen year old shouldn't be going sixty miles an hour."

Frank sensed Wally's anger and his concern, but thought he was overreacting.

"What makes you think he was going sixty miles an hour, Wally?"

"Because I followed him in my aeroplane!"

Needless to say, Kevin was grounded for a week, and just in case this was not enough deterrent, we threatened that the bike would be sold should we ever again hear about such dangerous speeds.

We never did hear any more biking reports, but today, almost twenty years later, he is still driving at break-neck speeds! We think he has found his niche this time, though. He's now burning up the track with his stock car where sixty miles an hour just isn't fast enough!

Kevin and his motorbikes

Heather Campbell

You Can't Escape the Long Arm of the Law

With our bags finally packed, our dream of visiting Australia was at long last going to become reality. To save us the worry and expense of airport parking, our son Kevin who was only nineteen at the time, volunteered to drive us to Ottawa, a ninety minute drive from our Beachburg home.

Upon arriving, Kevin helped us get our bags into the airport and then went to find a parking spot while we fretted about flight details. Later Kevin met us in the snack bar and, over coffee, we visited and gave him final instructions about taking care of the house while we enjoyed a vacation in Australia. All too soon it was time to proceed to the fenced off departure section. Waving one last good bye, we watched as Kevin headed back to the car and then we found a seat for our final wait.

Trying to ignore Frank's obvious nervousness, I settled into the novel I had brought to read. This was to be Frank's first flight and he could not relax. I'm sure every possible thing that could go wrong on this twenty-one hour flight was playing through his mind. He began pacing, back and forth, back and forth. Suddenly, over the loud speaker came this announcement; "Would Frank Campbell please come to the security desk? Frank Campbell, to the security desk, immediately, please."

"What the..," Frank muttered, feeling his jacket pocket just to make sure he still had his passport. I was holding our tickets and by now I was in a state of high anxiety too.

" I guess they just want you, not me," I said feebly. "What do you suppose it's all about?"

"Who knows? We'll probably miss our flight." Frank always imagined the worst, but this time I was inclined to agree with him.

I watched as he left the departure section, straining to see where he went. Then I could see in the distance Kevin striding towards him. Now my heart really did begin pounding. Had he had an accident? Why was he back here in the airport instead of on his way home? The two of them met. I could see Frank shaking his head. At one point they looked my way, but of course Kevin was not allowed into the departure zone, nor was I allowed out. Frank was now rubbing his forehead in the way he does when he's thinking through a problem. I was trying to read the body language. How big a problem was it? Kevin looked unscarred. What could it be if it was not an accident?

Finally Frank turned to come back and Kevin took out his wallet as he walked away. I waited.

"Our car has been impounded by the R.C.M.P.!" Frank announced when he got within earshot. I saw heads jerk in our direction, followed by curious glances and unvoiced questions.

"Our car has been impounded!" I repeated in disbelief. "Why?"

"Apparently you forgot to renew your license plate."

"Oh, my God! When should I have done that?"

"Your last birthday."

I turned that bit of information over in my mind. It was now July. My last birthday was in October. "You mean I have been driving illegally since October and they're just now catching up with me?"

"That's right. Nine months."

"Well, this sure was great timing! And just what do these fellows plan to do about getting Kevin home?" I asked in total innocence.

Frank looked at me with almost a pitying look. "They're not going to do a thing. The car is being towed away. It's up to Kevin to find a way home. The car sits here until he can come back with the licence plate and the money for the fine and a cheque to cover the storage fee."

"You've got to be kidding?" I exclaimed, knowing full well that he wasn't. "That doesn't make any sense. Is it that big a crime?"

"Apparently so. I guess business must be slow," Frank admonished.

"Poor Kevin! What's his plan?"

"Well, he's going to see if he can get Jeff on the 'phone. Hopefully he can come from Beachburg and get him."

And so that was Ottawa's gift to us as we left for a trip that would take us to the furthest destination away possible. We had hoped to leave with a carefree feeling; instead, we were leaving "carfree"!

Kevin, thanks to friend Jeff, did get home safely after waiting almost two hours while Jeff made the trip. Within three days he had the required paperwork and could rescue our car. The cost: Two trips to Ottawa, two hundred dollars in fines, much sweat and anxiety, and several phone calls back and forth from Australia. As if that wasn't bad enough, I also had my luggage searched at Australian Customs, but that's another story.

The Returned Prodigal

With so many parents experiencing the return to the nest of at least one of their adult-fledglings, we need guidance. *The Parable of the Prodigal Son, Book 2*, could be a best seller!

After the biblical parents put shoes on his feet, clothes on his back, and killed the fatted calf, how long did the glad rejoicing with no questions asked continue?

Our son has been living away from home for the past two years, enjoying college life and the automotive technician course. When he left us, he eagerly looked forward to apartment-sharing, no curfews and "doing his own thing". It was going to be heaven-like to be away from the ever-watchful parental eye. Did he not realize that perhaps that parental-eye would too be sampling paradise?

In the beginning months, holiday visits home brought tales of college escapades and the great nightlife. But gradually these tales waned and we heard comments like "It's sure good to sleep in my own bed" and "Boy, that was a good supper, Mom." Somehow over those two years, the "good life" paled in comparison to being at home. As graduation approached, we noted some talk about getting a job near home, maybe even living at home!

Now it has finally happened. The prodigal son has returned home! Having a feast and celebration to mark the occasion as in the Bible wasn't really necessary. There are other incidents that proclaim his return. I no longer have a roll of masking tape in my drawer. The cutlery tray has fewer knives. The cupboard shelf has fewer mugs and tumblers.

Where are these items? They are in our garage where our graduate mechanic works evenings and weekends on all kinds of engines and machines! Those out-of-date shirts and the well-worn towels that had been designated for cottage life have marched to the garage as wipe-rags. My scrub pail is half-full of oil. The milk bill has tripled, not to mention an increased grocery bill, and the sink is clean only on Thursdays, the cleaning lady's day!

I meanwhile have earned my master's degree, *master of grease and oil stain removal*, that is. Coveralls seemingly don't cover all. My suspicions suggest that often those coveralls are still hanging on the back of the garage door, only to be donned after the first spot offers a reminder.

Last week when I decided it was time to clean the goldfish tank, I couldn't find the siphon that I use.

"Have you seen the siphon that I use to drain the dirty water from the fish tank?" I asked my in-residence mechanic.

"Oh, I meant to tell you Mom, I used it for sucking the antifreeze out of the cylinders of my car."

Somehow I doubt that the goldfish will understand why they are still swimming in polluted water!

Today I could not find my turkey baster. At least I'm getting smarter as to where to look, although I could not imagine what a mechanic with at least a thousand dollars worth of tools would want with a turkey baster! Yes, it was in the garage. It had been used for sucking fuel out of the skidoo tank!

To give credit where credit is due, our prodigal has offered to pay board. Do I accept his offer? Or should the "rejoicing and celebrating" continue indefinitely? After all, he is our son.

Alas – I don't think I can wait for *Book 2*. Finding those fish worms in a salad container in the fridge has pushed me to the brink! He'll pay – at least enough to cover the milk bill and the utensils that I must replace.

Perhaps too, having that cold hard cash in my hand will lessen my urge to evict this loved one the next time the shock of cold hard porcelain in the wee hours of the morning reminds me that it is once again necessary to check as to whether the seat was left up or down!

Heather Campbell

(Original version of the previous story was first printed in The Ottawa Citizen in 1989.)

My Single Mother Adventure

Years ago, when our son Kevin was about twelve, he and I traveled from our home in Ontario to Canada's west coast. Because husband Frank was unable to go, we left with mixed feelings of anticipation and fear. Although we'd had a few major trips as a family, I had never ventured far without Frank. In fact I had never been west of Ontario.

The first week was perfect. We flew to Calgary where we were met at the airport by relatives. Staying with them provided all the comforts of home and the camaraderie too. Neither Kevin nor I will ever forget the thrill of seeing the Calgary Stampede.

Then, as prearranged, we boarded an excursion bus for a tour that would take us to British Columbia. Our first glimpse of the Rockies filled us with awe. We just couldn't get enough of their majesty. The highway at times was a real cliffhanger, but we were so well looked after inside the bus that we felt safe and secure.

Once we had arrived in Vancouver though, we were on our own. The guided tour ended at the bus terminal. I had pre-booked a hotel room for us and, along with our luggage, we were deposited by taxi in its beautiful lobby.

Kevin was tired and wanted to go immediately to his room. Unfortunately I had other ideas. Our cash was starting to dwindle. I had had time during the bus trip to study the guidebook, which listed government-approved lodgings. Directly across the street from where we were now standing was a hotel that seemingly offered the same features for twenty dollars less. I phoned from the lobby. Yes, they had a vacancy. I booked it, sight unseen, and immediately cancelled the present one. It was early in the afternoon so there was no problem other than Kevin grumbling as he picked up the heavy bags to move them to the hotel across the street. He could see no need for this. I told myself I was the mother and knew what was best.

Perhaps the threadbare condition of the lobby carpeting

should have caused me to rethink this move, but I was still congratulating myself on having saved twenty dollars. The room itself was quite suitable, more of a suite than a bedroom. Kevin quit his grumbling when he saw that he was to have his own space. In fact, he immediately stretched out and fell asleep.

Meanwhile I gathered up our dirty laundry and headed for the elevator that took me to the laundry room on the bottom floor. The room was just off the underground parking garage. As I sorted our dirty clothes and filled the machines, I had time to observe hotel customers coming and going from the hotel to the parking. I began to feel a little nervous when I noticed that the men arriving there mainly wore black leather jackets, many chains and tattoos, and had physiques that suggested that they worked out every day.

I wasn't long in deciding that I would not stay in that deserted laundry room to dry the clothes. I took them directly from the spin cycle of the washer to our room and hung the wet wardrobe on chair backs, the shower curtain rod, and all of the lampshades. It was quite a sight. But it was not nearly as unique as the sight I had been introduced to on the ride back in the elevator! I was still reeling from the perfume worn by a heavily made-up brunette who was attired in the skimpiest, tightest, purple satin outfit that I had ever seen. Naïve as I was then, I still had not figured out the whole truth of my new lodging.

A little later I became aware of constant traffic outside our room's door. I started to keep watch through the card-size window in our door. Never had I seen so much green, orange, and purple satin, not to mention black leather. I guess what finally brought me to my senses was realizing what a short time these people were spending in their rooms. About every thirty minutes it seemed one person would be leaving and another would be coming soon after. I could see only four rooms from our closed door but that was enough. There was no way I would be opening that door again tonight! In spite of the commotion, my innocent son was still fast asleep. By now my mouth was dry, my hands clammy, and my heart was doing a syncopated rhythm.

Enough of this stong, independent, single mother approach! I dialed Frank in Ontario. The clock on my wall said 11:30 P.M. Not until I heard Frank's voice thick with sleep hundreds of miles away, did I remember about the time zone difference. It was 2:30 A.M. in Ontario!

"Frank," I whispered, "I'm in a hotel here in Vancouver and I think it's a whore house."

"Why are you whispering?" he asked.

"Because they're right outside my door and I don't want them to know I'm awake."

"Who's outside your door?"

"The men and women who do business here." My heart was pounding so hard that I could hardly get the words out.

"Well, where is Kevin?"

"He's asleep. He doesn't even know I've called you. What am I going to do?" At this point I think I was close to the breaking point.

"Well, no one's going to hurt you if you keep your door locked. Go to bed and then get yourself out of there and to a decent hotel in the morning. There's not much I can do from here."

Well, I knew that was right but the sound of his voice was so comforting that I hated to say good-bye. I thanked him for listening and apologized for waking him. I assured him I would call him again in the morning.

Any of you moms reading this will understand when I tell you that I did not sleep one wink that night. As soon as it was dawn I grabbed all the damp laundry from its various perches, stuffed it in a bag, woke the unsuspecting Kevin, trying to explain the situation in terms I hoped a twelve-year old could handle, and called a taxi. The hotel was quiet at that hour, but I assured Kevin that I had not had a dream!

It was at least a year later before I could look back on this adventure and laugh, and admit to anyone that I had taken my twelve-year-old son to a whorehouse to spend the night!

The Power of Association

Frank and I had been visiting various dealerships, shopping for the best buy on a lawn tractor. I am not very mechanically minded but had done my best to absorb every bit of information given by the sales people.

Unfortunately, our son, a mechanic by trade, had not been able to come with us. We needed his advice. When we returned home I was anxious to share with him the outstanding features of each model and get his opinion before we made the purchase.

Putting a coloured brochure in front of him, I pointed to one of the tractors and proudly announced, "The salesman said that this model costs more but is really the best buy because it is one of the few having oil tits."

Much to my chagrin, our son convulsed in laughter. I joined him, my face appropriately crimson, when my husband politely explained that the correct term was "grease nipples".

Aging and Me!

Yesterday as I prepared for my bath in our tiny cottage bathroom, I caught a glimpse of my naked self in the full-length mirror someone had leaned against the wall. Boy, that mirror definitely has to find a new home! Maybe one of those circus sideshows could use it.

Since there is definitely more to aging than just focusing on my physical appearance (thank goodness!), let's consider other aspects of aging. Shall we go to the mind? How many brain cells do we lose in a day? Do we grow new ones once we pass the age of fifty? My experience would convince me that they must grow very slowly. I used to be so proud of the fact that I was capable of multitasking. Any mother who also holds down a fulltime job has to be able to handle more than one thing at a time. It used to be no problem for me to be doing the laundry, cooking a meal, talking on the phone, and giving nods in answer to my kids' questions all at the same time. I could never understand why my husband could handle only one task at a time. Well, somewhere along the way I seem to have gained a whole bunch of testosterone. No, I don't mean I'm growing whiskers, well maybe one or two, but what I mean is if I try to do more than one thing at a time, you can be sure one of those things will turn out to be a disaster. Trying to multi-task now is also dangerous. Take for instance the time that I started running my bath, thought about the meat I needed to take out of the freezer, went to do that, noticed as I passed the computer that an e-mail had come in, sat down to attend to that and, you guessed it, temporarily forgot about my bath water. That was the closest thing to a flood that I've seen in a while.

It seems that I cannot hold a thought for longer than a nano-second. How many times lately have I found myself hurrying from one room to another to get something and then having no idea what that something was? Once recently, I arrived at a social function and realized that I had not put my earrings on. I could distinctly remember being in the bathroom and telling myself that as soon as I was finished combing my hair, I'd go to the bedroom for my earrings. What happened to that thought? It must have escaped with the hair that I'm losing more of these days.

Experience has taught me that it's no longer wise for me to change the location of any of my belongings. As sure as I move something that has occupied the same spot for its lifetime, then the very next time I want it I spend hours, sometimes days, tracking it down. Maybe I should start leaving a change of address card on the hallowed spot where said article had been! Yes, I'm beginning to understand why it's so difficult to teach an old dog new tricks!

And if I think of something I want to contribute to a conversation, I have been known to grab a pen and scratch a word on my hand. Otherwise, whenever I get my chance to talk, I have no idea what that important thought was. Why do I write on my hand? Because by the time I find a paper, that thought I had will probably have left me. At least I now have empathy for my mother who for years kept interrupting people mid-sentence with her thoughts.

Lately, before I phone anyone, I make jot notes if there is more than one thing about which I'm phoning. It's frustrating, but I've learned not to try and swim upstream. More than ever I comprehend what "go with the flow" means.

Enough said about the mind. Let's move below the head. Several years ago I made the acquaintance of "Arthur", you know, Arthur Itis. Raking, vacuuming, squatting to clean the fridge or to see what's in the bottom of the cupboard really upsets Arthur. My medicine cabinet is beginning to look like a pharmacy because of Arthur. Although each joint in my body knows him well, he is not welcome. When he visits, each of these joints painfully protests.

Every cloud does have a silver lining though. Never having liked housework anyway, I hire someone else to do more and more of the cleaning and heavy jobs so that Arthur will keep quiet. I am learning to accept my limitations and ask for help if it's not offered for carrying groceries. I think I'm getting the hang of what that expression "aging gracefully" means.

For the first time in my life, I am taking the odd afternoon nap and I have read more books this past year than in any year of my life, with the exception of university years. I have been able to rid myself of that nagging "you should be doing something feeling". I *am* doing something. I'm reading. Leave me alone.

The brightest silver lining to this aging cloud is that my kids now ask for my advice. Years ago I wondered if I'd ever be wise. It seems, in my kids' eyes anyway, I must be getting close.

The government recognizes us too if we live long enough. That Canada Pension at 60 years of age followed by the federal pension in five years is a bonus. I've also learned to appreciate the businesses that already give me a senior discount and I look forward to even more of this once I reach the magic age of 65. Granted, I needed these discounts more in the years I was raising a family, but again, I'll go with the flow.

I realize that I have mellowed as the years rolled along. Friends and family are far more important to me now than the material things of life. In fact, right now I wish I did not have so many material things. Clutter is becoming a problem. If I don't do something about it soon, it will be a problem for my kids when I am knocking on the *pearly gates*. I suppose I am justified in leaving them some clutter when I think of the years I dealt with theirs.

As far as the *pearly gates* are concerned, I hope I'll find all my friends there and we'll all be wrinkle-free, fat-free, pain-free, and completely free of the worry of what age has in store for us.

Heather Campbell

Campbells and the "Down Under"

Visiting Australia in August is paradise, well worth the twenty-one hour flight from Ottawa. We spent three weeks there a few years ago and I long to return.

Our good friends, Andy and Georgina, met us at the airport in Cairns, Queensland. We reveled in the warmth and the beauty. Even at the airport our learning about "the land down under" began as we realized that a mountain range fringed the far rim of the runway. Why had we thought that Queensland was flat?

Our twenty-one days there were filled with wonderment and curiosity. Did you know that washcloths are not part of the average Australian home? *Having some tucker* is eating a meal, and *a jumper* is a sweater. *Gidday-mate* is the common greeting. To complain is *to winge* and *fair-dinkum* means a thing is good. Wedges of cooked pumpkin are served as a vegetable with almost every meal at a restaurant.

Never to be forgotten was the thrill of holding a baby koala at the Featherdale Wildlife Park, and finally seeing the wombat, the platypus, the kangaroos and wallabies, and the Tasmanian Devil, animals that I had until then seen only in books and movies. Eucalyptus, the food of the koala, was abundant, as were many different kinds of gum trees. Yes, kookaburras really do sit in gum trees and their laughing is most entertaining.

We spent almost a week visiting with Andy and Georgina in Mackay, Queensland and seeing the local sights there. Even the ride from the airport was exhilarating as we tried to adjust to being on the *left* side of the road and to the top-notch speed that Andy drove on the narrow, winding roads he chose.

Seeing the sugar cane plantations, touring a sugar refinery, and visiting a banana plantation were unique experiences. Up until that time we had not been aware that a banana plant produces only one bunch of bananas per season, but that bunch may have as many as one hundred bananas. Each bunch is covered with a colourful plastic tarp to prevent it from any type of pests.

Dear Hearts and Gentle People

The boat trip on the Daintree River in Queensland gave us a taste of what the tropics can offer, complete with crocodiles.

Another day we visited The Great Barrier Reef. We were content to view the beautiful and varied coral from the glass-bottomed boat but did envy those who were confident enough to don snorkeling gear and be part of the coral display in the ocean beneath.

Eventually we left our friends in Queensland, boarded a small domestic plane and headed for "the great outback". The "school-of-the-air" in Alice Springs in the Northern Territory is probably a one-of-a-kind operation. We viewed the teacher at her radio-control post. She was in touch with her pupils who were living miles apart from one another. No central school could accommodate them because the bussing would take hours. Technology has so advanced that since our visit we have learned that television and computers now make the "school-of-the-air" even more available.

Author examining one bunch of bananas

From here we took a four-day bus trip through the red desert area of the Northern Territory. Kangaroos were everywhere. The *roo-catcher* attached to the front of the bus was there, as inhumane as it sounds, to deflect them. Here and there we waved to Aborigines, the native peoples of Australia, who seemed unconcerned and unimpressed with our greeting. As if the outside sights were not enough excitement, we had an "on-bus drama" in which a fellow passenger went into convulsions and did not respond. The bus driver contacted the "doctor-of-the-air" who takes care of the outback inhabitants only to be told that the doctor was already out on a mission. An air ambulance was summoned and our passenger was airlifted to a hospital.

We couldn't help but wonder if this passenger's attack had been caused by his climb up Ayers Rock only hours before. This is a 348 metre high monolith sitting like a huge loaf of bread that has been set out to cool on the flat plain that stretches out around it. Tourists flock to it and the adventurous ones welcome the ninety-minute challenge it offers of climbing to its peak. Although some of our tour group conquered this feat, the two of us did only part of the climb and returned to the bottom to tour its base. On the side opposite to the climb we discovered bronze plaques engraved with the names and dates of those who had died in their attempts to climb Ayers Rock! Now why isn't this part of the tourist brochures I wonder!

    We endured the hot, rough desert trip for the rest of the day in anticipation of our next big stop, the opal mines of Coober Pedy, advertised as the opal capital of the world. What a jolt this was to what we had expected! Dotting the landscape here and there were huge holes with rickety fences around each. Nearby sat rusting trucks and primitive winches. Yes, there were opals in the ore but the ore was simply shoveled into buckets that were then attached to grappling hooks and hoisted up above ground to be added to huge piles already there. Oversized sieves operated by hand in a process called *noodling* sifted out the good material and it was trucked away. The only operation I could compare it with is what we had seen at Oak Island in Nova Scotia, Canada, where equipment was rusting, primitive-looking, and slow. The difference is that the opals extracted are valuable and supply world markets whereas Oak Island's gold has never been found.

    The Coober Pedy village near this site was novel and memorable. Most of the living quarters were below ground in what were called "dugouts". In this way the people escape the extreme heat of summer and the bitter cold of winter. We toured one of these houses, which had the basic comforts of home except that the walls were simply the hard soil whitewashed. The church, constructed in this same fashion but with some embedded stonework, was beautiful. Once inside you forget that you are underground, until someone turns off the lights! We had an opportunity to stay overnight in the underground rooms that "The Desert Cave Hotel" offers, but the experience with the lights off convinced me that I would be more content in the air-conditioned rooms above ground.

    By the time our bus reached Adelaide in Southern Australia, we were ready for pampering. The previous night we had endured the coldness that only the desert can offer at night and the discomfort of sleeping sitting upright on the bus.

From Adelaide we flew to Sydney in New South Wales, Australia's oldest and most populated city, where we spent a carefree four days exploring Australia's culture and history. We were amused as residents wrapped themselves in coats and shivered as they hurried off to work. In our short sleeves, we were enjoying what we thought was balmy weather. Shop keepers would nod and say, "Canadians, eh?"

We took a guided bus tour of the city, becoming acquainted with the area known as "The Rocks", and seeing the famous Opera House, the harbour and the Harbour Bridge on which Paul Hogan (Crocodile Dundee) had once worked as a painter.

On our last night there we treated ourselves to a show at a nightclub. No visit is complete without hearing a didgeridoo player. Originally this was an Aborigine instrument made from a hollowed tree trunk, but other musically-inclined citizens have adopted it. The sound produced by blowing into this instrument is so haunting and so unique.

Regretfully it was time to leave behind the many landscapes, climates, and attractions that Australia offers. We taxied to Sydney Airport well in advance of our departure time and paid the required departure tax that would allow us to leave the country, a concept I have never quite understood. Checking my watch when we had taken care of the necessities, I groaned at realizing we had so much waiting time. Frank had settled into a book. I wished I had some magazines and so I headed for the souvenir shop.

Souvenirs always speak to me, and I spent a while deciding whether or not I should buy any, and then some more time in selecting my magazines and some postcards. Suddenly I realized that Frank was at my elbow and his tone was urgent. "Get out of here or we are going to miss our plane." I felt he was exaggerating but I did pay for my few purchases as quickly as I could and then went to join him in the departure line.

"This line doesn't look too long," I thought to myself. That was before we stepped around a partition that I thought would put us at the departure door. Instead I saw an endless line of people ahead of us. By then the loudspeaker was calling our flight number. Frank checked his watch. "We are going to miss our flight!" he said with certainty. I was speechless and suddenly felt faint and guilty. We still had to be checked through security with all items placed in the conveyor belt and then picked up again on the other side. Finally we reached the last ticket checker who looked at our tickets and said, "You'd better run. Your plane leaves in three minutes!"

Frank was wearing the large akubra (cowhand hat) that we had bought for our son and toting both carry-on bags. I had only my purse and so I ran ahead reaching the passenger stairs just as the attendant was preparing to have them folded up. I showed her my ticket and breathlessly explained that my husband was behind me. We both looked back to see Frank trying to run with a heavy bag in each hand and yet not lose the akubra perched on his head. In retrospect we can laugh but the situation was too tense at the time. The door of the plane literally did close on our heels and we were hurried to our seats.

Although I would have been happy to stay in Australia for more sightseeing, I wasn't anxious to lose the price of my ticket. It took me at least a half hour to regain my composure and it was then that I realized that my magazines and postcards must still be on the airport's conveyor belt at the security check. All that careful shopping and nothing to show for it!

Well, that's not quite true. Many years have passed but each time I see that akubra, the memory surfaces of Frank laden down and trying to keep this on his head. I smile to myself as I replay so much of our trip in my mind. Magazines eventually get thrown out but fond memories stay with us forever.

Dear Hearts and Gentle People

*Mining Equipment at Coober Pedy
Note the mining shaft in the foreground.*

Noodling, hoping to find opals in the discarded ore

Entertainers at the Argyle Tavern, Sydney, Australia

Note the didgeridoo in the foreground.

Opera House, Sydney Harbour, Australia

Dear Hearts and Gentle People

Judging a Cookie By Its Cover

I was shopping at five o'clock, "the witching hour", when everyone including me is so hungry. In my case it should be called the "wishing hour" – wishing that supper would be ready when I would bomb through the door at home.

I had my grocery list in-hand and was dutifully following it, that is until I passed the long array of packaged cookies. The big sign advertising "Mrs. Field's Cookies, regularly $4.29, now $2.99" caught my eye. Towering over the sign were bright red boxes shaped almost like gift bags and showing a choice of either mouth-watering chocolate chip or macadamia nut cookies. Normally I detest commercially packaged cookies, which are usually hard and dry, but these looked so promising. Along with this tantalizing cookie picture, the name Mrs. Field convinced me a farmer's wife had just popped these into a box ready for the Campbell's table. Into my cart went the chocolate chip variety and I hurried on with my list.

Driving home I was mentally planning our supper. The winter weather always makes me even hungrier. Thank goodness for last night's leftovers to warm up. Added to that, tonight we would have cookies with our tea, a special treat.

In record time I had the groceries unpacked, the leftovers warmed, and Frank and I were eating supper. Once we had finished the main course, I ushered in the prize package of cookies. I handed Frank an empty plate and the bag to be opened as I poured us each a cup of tea. He carefully opened the top perforation, peered inside, looked at me in a puzzled manner, and then slid a plastic tray out of the package. He sat the tray on the table and we both stared in total disbelief. No, we weren't staring at the cookies. They still were in disguise, each one wrapped in a sealed, white foil envelope. What was unbelievable was the meagre amount, a total of eight cookies! I was glad we did not have any guests for supper. How far would eight cookies have gone?

I realized, after some quick mental math, that if I had paid regular price, each cookie would have cost 54 cents, plus tax!

Were they good? So far we each have eaten only one. I

thought it was very tasty but my spouse's comment was, "It's nothing that I couldn't live without."

I'm certainly glad that he felt that way. Mrs. Field may have to look "far afield" for future customers as far as I am concerned!

On the other hand, maybe I should investigate the start-up costs for Mrs. Campbell's cookies!

Tradition! Tradition!

"Without our traditions, our lives would be as shaky as a fiddler on the roof", the philosophizing Tevye sings in the popular "Fiddler On the Roof" production. Although we were never as adamant as Tevye, over the years my family has faithfully honoured a few traditions, especially birthday celebrations. I credit my mother with setting the stage for this. From the earliest time that I can remember, every birth date in our family was acknowledged each year with a festive meal and gifts. Up until I was about twelve, there would be an afternoon party too, with invited guests from my age group.

From the teen years on there never was an actual party, but the family still celebrated. Mom always made the cake. Before she baked it she would wrap symbolic treasures in wax paper and poke them into the batter. The gooey mixture would bake up around these little bundles and hide them completely. I remember unwrapping such things as a button, a toothpick, a coin, or a ring. The button meant that you were going to be a bachelor or a spinster (which we referred to as "old maid"); the toothpick suggested that you would work hard for your living and be poor; the ring meant that you would be married soon; and the coins, of course, meant that you would accumulate wealth in proportion to whatever size of coin it was. Mom always included several coins of different denominations.

Depending on how the cake was sliced, sometimes you would be served a piece of cake with nothing in it. That was always disappointing when you were a child. On the other hand, it meant that you deserved another piece of cake. Mom's cakes were always two-layers with frosting or jam holding them together and more frosting on the outside. Sometimes the cake was chocolate, sometimes white, sometimes angel food, but always delicious. On the top would be the exact number of candles to match your years. Not until I was well into my twenties had anyone ever heard of ordering a bakery cake. Tim Horton's did not exist. Frugality was an ingrained habit.

Parties in my childhood years meant playing indoor games. A favourite was " pin the tail on the donkey". A blindfold was put over your eyes and a paper donkey tail with a pin stuck in one end was thrust into your hand. Someone grabbed your shoulders and spun you around about three times, expecting you to walk straight ahead to where a donkey shape had been taped to the wall and pin that tail in the proper spot. Everyone shrieked and hooted as you fumbled around in your blind state, finally stabbing that pin into the spot where you thought that tail belonged. When ripping off your blindfold, you usually realized how far off the mark you had been. Of course the person who stabbed the closest to that donkey's rear won a prize.

Going to the local laser-maze, arcade, ski-hill, or bowling alley, as children do now for birthday parties, was not even in the dream-stage in those days. Video rentals were unheard of. We made our own entertainment.

The best part for the celebrity was the gift opening. In my earliest years, the most common gift to receive was a colouring book and crayons. Girls also liked to receive books of cutouts. The heavy book cover usually contained the male or female shape to cut out and the pages inside were the clothes to be cut out. Each outfit had little tabs at the shoulders that you folded over to fasten these clothes to the body. Boys, of course, liked to receive toy guns. At that time, playing with toy guns was not frowned upon. Children imitated what they saw in the "wild-west" movies. Granted, my dad forbid me to join the boys in these games, but only because he did not think it was lady-like.

By the time I had children of my own in the late sixties, Barbie dolls had replaced cutouts, but guns still proved popular with the boys.

As we matured, the gifts carried less significance than the

celebration itself, at least in my family. Although we had our own parties at home for the kids, Mom loved to have the whole family get together again so that she and Dad could be part of the celebration. I have a special bond with my nephew, Steven, who never had the limelight to himself, but always had to share with me because our October birthdays are only two days apart.   Mom's cake, served with ice cream, was always the focal point. Photos were taken centred around the cake. We soon learned that none of us looked too glamorous posed like a blowfish trying to extinguish all the candles. Our photo albums are full of snapshots of birthday get-togethers. One friend shook her head and remarked that we were the most picture-taking family she had ever seen. Perhaps she was right.

I hate to think that some day these albums will be discarded. Somehow each year, as children become adults, and the family becomes more scattered, these pictures are more appreciated by me. Although only rarely now can the extended family get together, I try to keep birthday celebrations alive in our immediate family. I find myself accepting the tradition-torch passed to me by Mom who is no longer able to be the bearer.

Great Grandma Hazel (author's Mom) shows Great Grandson Sam her 88th birthday cake as Mark (dad) and Grandma Maureen look on.

Dear Hearts and Gentle People

Sharing Our October Birthday Cakes

Nephew Steven and Author Heather

*Nephew Chris, Brother Allyn,
Nephew Steven and Author Heather*

Dear Hearts and Gentle People

A Night On The Town

My husband and I were delighted when we read in the paper that Roger Whittaker, long a favourite singer of ours, would be entertaining at the National Arts Center in Ottawa. We had no trouble in convincing some of our friends that we all should go. Since there were ten of us, the trip necessitated taking two cars. We decided that each carload would do their own thing in the way of shopping, but we'd all meet for dinner in the NAC restaurant, and then proceed to the concert.

Lorna and Eric along with Kenny and Darlene arrived at the restaurant first. They explained that they were part of a group of ten, and wanted to wait for the rest to arrive. Because we all wanted to sit together, they were granted permission to rearrange the furniture to accommodate us all. Then they waited – and waited- and waited. Periodically either Kenny or Eric would go out and check the adjacent streets, just in case the rest of us were having trouble finding our way.

Alas, they didn't check the parking garage. What a pity!

Our carload had had a pleasant drive to Ottawa, the men in the front seat and the women in the back so that we could all visit. When the car was finally parked in the underground parking, everyone got out, everyone except me that is! I couldn't get my seatbelt undone. Try as I might, the clasp just wouldn't budge. I was a prisoner in my own car!

At first we laughed. In the ensuing minutes, each person had a try at unbuckling the stubborn belt.

"Try wiggling out," my husband suggested.

"Frank, I'm all dressed up. Even if I weren't, what kind of a contortionist would I have to be to get myself out of this by wiggling? I'd probably end up strangling myself."

By now the tears of laughter ruining my mascara were becoming tears of frustration.

Neil, who usually carries a jackknife, searched his pockets, but then realized that he probably hadn't transferred the knife to these good trousers. What were we going to do?

"The rest of us could go ahead, and send you down a sandwich, Heather," one of them suggested.

"You are all just full of good ideas," I grumbled, trying to manage a smile.

None of us knew how to get a message to the "would-be diners" who were saving our seats upstairs in the restaurant. By now we knew that they would be starting to worry. Our own worry was approaching the panic stage. Suddenly I remembered that a few weeks ago I had stuck a pair of school scissors in the glove compartment, planning to work on a craft project at home that I wanted to introduce to my pupils in an art lesson. I had never done it and so the scissors must still be there.

Frank unlocked the glove compartment, rifled through the papers and voila! - the scissors!

Seatbelts are made to last, so it took a little extra effort with these very ordinary scissors, but finally the belt was in two pieces and I was released!

We hurried upstairs to the restaurant where four very hungry and very relieved friends actually cheered when they saw us.

The evening had been saved. Our dinner was a bit rushed but the concert was wonderful. I was so thankful not to have had to spend the time confined in my seatbelt, staring at the scenery in the parking garage!

The scissors are now a very permanent fixture in our car. For a long time afterwards I was so paranoid that I even carried a little fold-up knife in my purse. Recently I bought a purse that came equipped with nail file and scissors. Taking my cue from the motto of the Boy Scouts, I now am *Always Prepared*.

Diane's Dilemma

Our friends, Diane and Ron, had enjoyed a summer auto trip out west. They had taken turns driving so that the trip could be enjoyed by each of them and neither of them would become too tired.

Upon arriving home a few weeks later, they basked for a few days in memories and self-congratulations on how well things had gone. That is until a letter arrived with a speeding ticket that had been issued through one of the western province's new photo I.D. system. Diane was furious with Ron. She waved the picture and letter in front of him and expounded on all the previous tickets he had had for speeding. When was he ever going to learn? Hadn't she reminded him enough times to slow down?

Ron was appropriately quiet through this tirade. He knew he was guilty of having too many speeding fines. When Diane had finally reached the end of her monologue, he said, "Let me see that letter."

For the last several years Ron has had to admit that he was approaching baldness at an alarming rate. As he looked at the picture that had been taken from the back-view, he was amazed at how much hair he had grown! Then he noticed that the ticket had been issued in the afternoon. A smile spread over his face. Diane was the one that had always driven after lunch.

He handed the letter back to Diane. "Honey, this is a picture of you at the wheel. It was taken at 2 o'clock on Tuesday. Welcome to the "speeders' club"!

Ron says it's strange how he has never heard another word about speeding tickets!

Clap! Clap!

We are friends with a wonderful couple, Lorna and Eric. Everyone has their foibles, and Lorna and Eric would be the first to admit that they are notorious for losing and misplacing their keys. Any kind of a key, whether it is for a motel room, a suitcase, a house, or an automobile can do a regular disappearing act with them. The time spent searching for the phantom key is frustrating and sometimes futile.

Enter the helpful sister-in-law, Darlene. She had discovered that key chains exist that can be summoned by the clap of your hands. They work on the same principal as the popular table lamps that can be activated from a distance if a person claps their hands together. This seemed the perfect gift to solve the "key problem" and that is what Lorna received as her Christmas gift from Darlene.

Having the car key and the house key on this chain did prove very useful at home. One clap and the beeping led them straight to that spot where they'd left them! It's peculiar how often we lay our keys down while we do something else, then walk away and forget all about them. Of course, clapping for your keys and having your pocket start beeping is a bit embarrassing!

But embarrassment reached a new height one day when Lorna went shopping at the mall. She was looking for a new outfit and, like most women, did not find it in the first dress shop. In fact she visited several in two hours. Finally she did find an outfit to her liking, made the purchase and, after tending to a few other items on her list, was ready to go home. Guess what! No keys. Now would be the time to clap and have that key chain beep, right? Well, maybe.

Try to picture a woman walking up and down the mall and, as discreetly as possible, clapping her hands together every few steps. Some people stared, others averted their glances, and some people looked with pity!

It would be nice if I could end this tale by saying that the key chain finally did answer and the embarrassing clapping had been worth it. Not so. The keys and the chain were gone forever. If someone clapped their hands near the mall's garbage bin very late that evening, they may have wondered if the bomb squad needed to be called! Modern technology isn't always foolproof.

The Pregnant Grandmother

A few years ago, when I was well into my fifties, I decided that the varicose veins in my legs were unsightly. Besides that, my legs throbbed if I stood too long. My doctor referred me to a specialist in Ottawa who used saline solution injected into the varicose veins to shrivel them up. Other veins took over the work. At least that was how I understood this medical procedure. I was assured by the specialist that this method had been used in France for a long time and was perfectly safe.

So I began driving the two-hour trip to Ottawa on a regular basis for the treatments. The burning sensation after the injections was annoying, but not unbearable. After each treatment, my legs were wrapped with heavy, elasticized bandaging and I was told to walk as much as possible in the next hour. Moving my legs would help to prevent any danger of clotting.

That was welcome advice. What better way to do the required walking than to go shopping? Touring a mall in Ottawa would be just what the doctor ordered!

I love company when driving any distance and so on one trip I took my friend Grace, whom I knew was another "born to shop" person. Once we reached the clinic I insisted that Grace get started on her shopping at the little mall nearby and we'd meet back at the van in an hour. All went as planned. My legs were bandaged, and I headed for the van where Grace was already waiting. It was time to get to the larger mall and get in all the prescribed walking!

I started the van, backed out of my spot, shifted to drive and tried to accelerate. Nothing happened. By now I was in the way of other parked vehicles. I shifted to park, turned off the ignition and restarted the vehicle. Once again it refused to go ahead. I got out to see how badly I was blocking traffic and to figure out what other options I might have. Fortunately, a young man who was sitting in a nearby vehicle had been watching, and was now walking towards me.

"It looks like you've got troubles. Do you mind if I see what I can do?"

"I'd be ever so grateful. I've never had this problem before."

So he got behind the wheel, but with no better results than I had had. Then he looked under the hood while I was at the wheel again.

"I'd say your transmission is finished. You'd better call someone. In the meantime I'll see if I can push you back into your spot here."

Thank goodness I had C.A.A. insurance. I went back into the clinic, called the given number, and within ten minutes a tow truck appeared.

I explained the problem and mentioned that we were two hours from home and that I sure hoped he could fix it today.

After a brief inspection, the young attendant informed me

that the transmission would have to be replaced and that the best that he could do was to hook on to the van and tow us home.

"All the way to Pembroke?" I exclaimed.

'That's correct. You have coverage for that."

"But the doctor has told me that for the next hour I should walk more than I sit so that the blood in my legs circulates well."

The attendant scanned me quickly, noting the wrapped legs I am sure.

"Well, I have to stop for a smoke once in a while. I'll let you out to walk each time. I hope that will be good enough."

I realized that my options were pretty limited and so I nodded in agreement.

"Where are we riding?"

"In the cab of the truck with me. It will be a little cozy but we'll manage."

And so Grace and I clambered into the cab, stepping over a car jack and nameless other equipment on the floor. We made ourselves as comfortable as possible as my van was being hoisted on behind.

The attendant was a good conversationalist and kept up a steady flow of chatter as we bounced along. I kept shifting my position as often as I dared, hoping that would help the circulation. Finally it was time for a smoke-break and we pulled into a rest stop. I slid out too and walked around, leaving Grace and our driver talking.

When we all got back into the cab, Grace said to me, "This young man wants to know how far along you are in your pregnancy."

I looked at her in disbelief and we burst out laughing. I turned to him and said, "You have made my day. I'm a grandmother and far too old to be having children, but it's so nice that you thought I was still that young." Then I explained about the varicose vein treatments.

He chuckled too. "Maybe you haven't noticed but I have been avoiding all the bumps that I could because of your pregnancy. You ladies are now in for a much rougher ride!"

Dear Hearts and Gentle People

Do You Have your Teeth?

"Do you have your teeth?" has become a pretty standard question for Lorna to ask Eric. She has good reason.

Our friend Eric has a dental appliance, often referred to as a bridge. Two back molars are attached to this bridge. As we all know, it is important for us to have these so that all our teeth keep their proper spacing. Eric has been advised by his dentist to remove the bridge at night and, unlike myself, he does this faithfully. Our gums need a chance to breathe is the dental philosophy. Eric's philosophy is that it is not often that he nibbles on anything in bed so he doesn't need them there!

A few years ago the four of us motored to Arizona together for a winter holiday. We stayed at several motels on the way there and again coming home. Each day we tried to cover as many miles as possible, especially on the return journey.

It was on our last morning on the homeward journey, about two hundred miles from the last night's motel, that I passed around some gum. I had no idea at the time what message this conveyed to Eric. I learned the revelation several days later.

Apparently Eric had put his dental appliance in a glass of water on the nightstand in our last motel, a customary practice by then. However, the practice of putting it back in his mouth in the morning never happened that day. Neither he nor Lorna noticed until I passed around the gum. People wearing appliances recognize gum-chewing as a challenge. Eric had a different challenge that morning. He had decided that none of us would be impressed by the fact that his teeth were sitting in a glass two hundred miles away. He was intent now on not revealing that they were missing. Since they were back molars, that task was relatively easy. None of us noticed.

Two days later Eric mentioned it to Lorna.

"Why didn't you say something sooner?" she asked.

"We were too far down the trail to turn back, especially in winter weather. Do you think we should phone the motel?" he asked.

Lorna figured by now the teeth had been tossed, but she

hunted around for their hotel receipt and found the telephone number. When she related their predicament to the desk-clerk, he asked, "Can you describe the teeth?"

"Why?"

"Because we have more than one set here," he laughed. I think Eric found that fact comforting. Other people had driven off toothless too.

So the appliance was described and the good news was that the teeth were still there and the management would ship them.

Weeks turned to months and no teeth arrived. Eric even checked at the Customs Office to see if perhaps the package with such unusual contents had been held up there. He was assured there was nothing there for him.

Six months later Eric had given up and was making plans for getting a new appliance when the unexpected happened. A misshapen and tattered box arrived in the mail. In spite of the unattractive wrapping, the appliance inside was intact! Gum-chewing was once more a challenge, but a welcome one!

※※※※※※※※※※※

Not long ago Eric and wife Lorna were visiting at their son's in Toronto for a grandchild's birthday. At bedtime Eric did his routine cleaning of his appliances (He had gained another one since the last story) and, for want of a tumbler, he wrapped each appliance in tissue and put each bundle safely on the back of the vanity. Then he returned to the living room to gather up the three grandchildren, who ranged in age from two to eight, and tuck them into bed.

After a little more visiting with the rest of the family, he and Lorna said their good-nights and headed for bed. As is customary, Eric made one more trip to the bathroom. This time he noticed that the grandchildren had not been very tidy in their frequent bathroom trips and there were many bits of tissue on the floor and on the sink. It would be best to clean it up he thought, and he did. He grabbed all the tissues, threw them in the toilet, and flushed.

Yes, you guessed it, not only had he flushed the tissue strewn by the children, but also the tissue containing his teeth. He realized it almost before the last sucking gasp of the flush had ended, but how do you stop a flush? To say Eric had a "sinking feeling" would be an understatement!

The confession took place at the breakfast table the next morning. You can imagine the jokes. "Gee Dad, I guess some fish in Lake Ontario has new dentures."

Upon arriving home, Eric made a dentist appointment and was overjoyed to learn that his insurance covers the cost of a new dental appliance every five years.

Since history does seem to repeat itself, to be on the safe side, I think for the next five years Eric needs a special carrying case for his troublesome ivories!

Love Those "Newfies"

When we were younger, we loved to see different parts of Canada on our holidays and we kept our costs down by tenting. By the 70's we had updated a bit and were the proud owners of a tent trailer that we towed behind our car. We'd see the sights through the day, pull into a campground by suppertime, hoist the tent and be set for the evening. It was a relief not to have to blow up air mattresses as we had done when all we had was a tent. While we cooked our supper or sat around a fire, we often chatted with other campers.

No conversation in all those years matches the one told to us by a fellow camper in P.E.I. who had the superior camping trailer of the time, a pop-up. By merely turning a crank, the tent set up before your eyes. Taking it down was just as easy; simply turn the crank in the opposite direction.

We had marvelled at the ease of it all.

"Well it is great, but let me tell you about an experience," the owner said.

"One morning not long ago in a campground where I knew no one, I got the wife and two kids up at 4 A.M. so we could have our breakfast and be on the road by 5A.M. None of us were too talkative at that hour of the morning. Of course, the kids wanted to sleep in, weren't hungry, and did not appreciate the beauty of seeing the sun rise. After a rather dismal breakfast, my wife and I packed up the dishes, put the kids in the car, and I proceeded to crank down the tent. Well, that crank was less cooperative than the kids! It wouldn't budge and so the tent sat upright on the trailer. Time was fleeting and I knew that if we didn't leave by five o'clock we would not keep to the schedule that we had planned. No one else was stirring at that hour in the campground. I had no one to offer assistance. I knew there was a service center about three miles away. By now both the wife and kids were lamenting the fact that they were in the car and ready and wondered what was taking so long." At this point he paused in his story, shaking his head as if the whole scene was replaying.

"I had no choice but to take off down that Trans Canada Highway, pulling that fully erect tent behind us and praying I would get to the service center with everything intact," he chuckled.

Frank and I were smiling just picturing that in our minds, but his story wasn't finished yet.

"Now can you imagine the jokes being made by other travelers out there on that busy highway?" At that point he stepped aside to reveal to us for the first time his licence plate. You guessed it, Newfoundland!

A Somewhat Smelly Tale

Frank's cousin Carol, who lives in Windsor, had an interesting experience one year when she visited her son in Arizona. At that time it was cheaper to drive to Detroit and fly from there than it was to get a flight out of Canada. All went well on the trip to Arizona and Carol enjoyed her week's visit. Too soon it was time to pack up the suitcase and board the plane back to Detroit. Because most of her clothes were dirty, Carol's packing consisted mainly of jamming all of the dirty clothes into her suitcase and adding her cosmetic bag and her last pair of clean socks.

Good-byes and hugs were exchanged all around and Carol boarded the morning plane with little incident. It was a good flight. She relaxed with a book and savoured the last few hours of her vacation. Tomorrow she would be back to work.

Dear Hearts and Gentle People

After landing in Detroit, Carol dutifully retrieved her suitcase from the airport's luggage carousel and hurried off to her car. It took awhile to get out of the congested parking lot but finally she was on her way. In one hour's time she was pulling into her own driveway in Windsor. Even though there was no one to greet her, it was good to be home.

Carol relaxed with a cup of tea and some stale cookies while savouring the sounds of her own abode. Then, remembering the dirty laundry, she fetched her suitcase from where she had dropped it at the doorway, carried it to the laundry room and opened it. "My God!" she yelled to the empty room. "Oh, my God!"

By this time she was laughing hysterically as she held up the most beautiful wedding dress she had ever seen. In the bottom of the suitcase were white wedding shoes and tucked in one pocket was a single strand of pearls.

Carol flopped the lid of the suitcase down. This luggage was identical to her own. She grabbed the handle and found the baggage tag on which a name and partial address had been scribbled, obviously in haste. She hoped that it would be enough to satisfy the airport's computer.

It was Friday. Would the owner be wanting this dress tonight? What kind of a panic must she be in? Carol doubted that this girl, whoever she was, would be bothering to wash Carol's clothes! More likely she'd feel like pitching, maybe even burning them!

Carol dialed the airport and explained the predicament. She was referred to "Customer Service". Yes, they already had had a very anxious and upset bride-to-be contact them. The wedding was tomorrow. If Carol could get the suitcase to them, the bride would pay whatever expense was involved in the transporting of it, as well as paying for her overnight accommodation.

Within an hour Carol was once again on the highway to Detroit. This trip was certainly an inconvenience and might cost her a day's pay but, being a woman, she understood that a young bride's happiness was at stake.

In spite of the seriousness of the situation, Carol giggled each time she imagined the scenario of the bride-to-be opening Carol's suitcase, expecting to find her beautiful, snow-white wedding dress, and instead being treated to the sight and odour of a week of dirty clothes! This was certainly a prime example of "airing your dirty laundry in public"!

Sometimes it's just not enough to be *wearing* clean underwear!

The Sun Doesn't Always Shine

Until a year ago, my brother Allyn owned a 1994 Sunfire. He put great faith, and sometimes hope, in his little Sunfire. Even though each morning he noticed that it needed several tries before it would start, he consoled himself with the fact that it always did start.

One Saturday morning as he and his wife Maureen arrived at Tim Horton's for their weekend ritual of coffee and a muffin, Maureen asked, "Do you think we should leave the car running while we're inside?"

"No, it's warmed-up now. It will start," Allyn declared.

Well, you've heard of famous last words. When they were ready to go back home, the little Sunfire wouldn't emit even a squeak or a promise. It seemed to have fired for the last time.

My brother, admittedly not being mechanically inclined, has always had the wisdom to belong to C.A.A. Back he went to the coffee shop, a telephone, and a coffee-to-go (hopefully).

The C.A.A. truck arrived. The young mechanic did a thorough tapping and testing, but "the fire" was definitely out! He couldn't get even a spark.

" I think you need a new starter. We'll have to tow it to a garage. I'll drop you two off at home on the way."

In a few hours the garage phoned Allyn to confirm that a starter was needed and gave him an estimate of the cost. Allyn gave the go-ahead; after all, what good is a car without a starter?

The next day the call came that the car was ready. Allyn was overjoyed. I guess the attendant assumed that he would be right there to pick it up so he left the car running.

Allyn arrived several hours later, jumped in the car, turned the key and there was no response. You guessed it. The car had quit and the running lights had drained the battery.

The young mechanic, who felt responsible for the problem, hurried out with a power pack used to start cars. Allyn never questioned him until there was a strong odour and still no charged battery. The poor lad had never been told that you don't start completely dead batteries with a power pack. Now the power pack was burnt up and the boss was on the scene! He was livid that an employee of his would do such a thing.

A truck and booster cables had to be summoned. Within minutes the Sunfire lived up to its name.

"Just leave it running," Allyn directed, " and I'll go inside with you and see what I owe you."

My brother is retired and seldom hurries. When he did finally get into his Sunfire and drive away, he went only the length of the parking lot and the car choked, gasped, and quit. Apparently the "sun" had set for the day!

"How can this be?" he said aloud to no one in particular. He scanned the symbols on the dash for a clue. When his eye reached the square saying "Fuel", he knew the problem! The hand was well below the "empty" line. I'm not sure how red his face was, but at least this was a problem that he could handle himself. Well, almost. He did have to get a gas can from the garage.

With fuel in the tank and the gas can returned, my brother's faith was restored as he beamed his "Sunfire" toward home. All in all, I'm sure the mechanics at that particular garage had a good tale to take home that night.

Canine Tales

Dear Hearts and Gentle People

The Real Story of Chief

In my first book "The Show Must Go On" I told what I knew about Dad's hound "Chief". I have since learned more.

First of all, my brother has verified that it was no accident that Chief so often escaped from his outdoor chain in the back yard. Dad had a hand in it, literally.

Chief was often seen about town and he always carried a piece of cardboard in his mouth. It was about a foot and a half square and wherever he stopped to rest, he would drop that piece of cardboard and sit on it. When he was ready to move on, he picked the cardboard up by his teeth and dragged it with him to his next resting spot. I've known many toddlers who had to take their favourite blanket wherever they went, but Chief was the only dog I ever heard of who carried his own security blanket.

Many families each fall were in the habit of buying half a beef from a local farmer. The individual cuts were wrapped in brown freezer paper and labeled as to whether they were steak, roast, stew, or hamburg. Frank and Muriel McCaw kept a locked wooden box in their back porch. In the winter they stored their overflow of meat there and transferred it to their indoor refrigerator freezer as space allowed.

Muriel has told me just exactly what transpired on that back porch one day. She and Frank were sitting at their kitchen table when they saw Chief making an exit from their back porch, carrying his cardboard, of course. Muriel jumped to see what damage he might have done. She noticed right away that the lid was slightly ajar on their meat locker and lying beside it was a badly torn wrapper labeled "sirloin steak". The thief was gone but the evidence remained.

She scolded herself for not having made sure the lid was locked and then returned to the kitchen where she reported to Frank that Howard Gunter's dog had helped himself to a choice cut, a sirloin steak!

Maybe because Frank and Dad were longtime hunting buddies, Frank just chuckled and said, "Gunter has him well-trained!"

As I said in my previous book, Chief was well-known by

the villagers, but not always well-loved.

Dream Dog

Each person's dream of retirement is different. My dream included having a dog. This was to be my companion dog, preferably a male and definitely a small size breed, the kind that would fit in my lap.

Two months after retiring from teaching, I noticed an advertisement in the local classifieds wanting homes for puppies. I read it out to my husband who surprised me by saying, "Let's go and look at them."

"Just remember," I warned, recalling his taste for large dogs, " it's a small dog I want."

Upon arriving at the given address, we were ushered into the kitchen and there beside the woodstove was a beautiful liver-coloured English Springer Spaniel mother and her litter of seven tiny pups. The mother was a little bigger than I had hoped but the pups were so adorable. I could sense my dream modifying somewhat as I held each one. The only male of the litter, a soft, black and white ball with curly ears, licked my hand affectionately.

There was no doubt that his mother was a purebred English Springer Spaniel, but what was his father? It seemed to be a case of address unknown, although the black and white Border Collie next door was suspect. This had definitely not been a planned pregnancy. The owners had hoped to raise purebred show dogs but someone neglected to bar the door a few months ago!

"I'm sure these pups will never be bigger than their mother," the owner declared. I looked at the mother and tried to picture her in my house and my dream. Not an exact fit, that was for sure.

"If you want a dog that is at home indoors or out, this is a wonderful breed," I was assured.

I picked up the cuddly black and white ball once more, and again he licked my fingers and then yawned contentedly. And so, as in other love affairs, the heart ruled the head. Ten minutes later we were driving home with our six-week old family member.

Our program of housebreaking and daily walks began. For the first week the word "no" became almost automatic, but by week two our puppy occasionally earned a "good boy", and the towel for mopping up accidents was being used a little less.

We named our new addition "Duffy" and he certainly became my dog, following me around the house on his wobbly legs. He loved to snuggle and for a few months he was indeed a lap dog. I walked him daily and even bought him a little coat so he wouldn't get a chill from the wind.

As Duffy grew, the English Springer Spaniel's characteristic long ears and sad eyes developed. But also developing at an alarming rate were four misfit long legs. One would think we had a colt! My dream dog, my lap dog, was a thing of the past, but the bond was too strong now to even consider finding him another home. Duffy was a permanent fixture.

Retired people do not stay at home much so it was good that I had a dog that liked the outdoors, even though, because of a town by-law, he had to be chained. I realized just how lonesome he must be outside when I heard him howling at each passing train. It wasn't long before the neighbor's normally quiet dog took up the habit too, and we had the "all-aboard" duet as the daily trains approached.

Springers really do spring. That is how Duffy greets me, in great giant leaps, and he is obviously so glad to see me that, no matter how tired or hurried I am, I give him the attention he so obviously expects. Sometimes I ask myself why my husband doesn't greet me with the same enthusiasm! There must be a lesson there somewhere.

A rather strange thing that Duffy does on a daily basis is what I call "herding". About ten o'clock each evening he checks on me to see whether I am watching T.V., typing, or in the kitchen. He paces around a couple of times and then flops down. In fifteen minutes or so he's on his feet again and trots down the hall and lies down beside the bed. He keeps repeating this performance until finally I do go to bed. He stays beside the bed until I turn out the light, and then he gets up quietly and leaves to find his own den. I think this "herding instinct" must be the Border Collie gene. Duffy's rounding up his cattle and herding them to the barn for the night.

No longer do we need an alarm clock. As soon as the sun is up I feel his wet nose against my face or hand. For the next fifteen minutes he prances and paces to signal that either Frank or I should be up. Finally, if we don't get up, he lands with all four feet on the bed. It's effective. As the sixty pounds of him crash beside me, I grope for my glasses and housecoat and bolt out of bed. Already he's ahead of me, doing his springing. His excitement about getting up this early is far greater than mine. He's to the door and back to check on me about three times before I get there to let him out. He does his watering routine outside and then heads back to the door demanding to be fed. Meanwhile I'm still at the coffee stage and not moving nearly as fast as he is. As soon as he has eaten, he flops down to sleep for the rest of the morning. His mission has been completed. "The cattle" are in the pasture. Some morning maybe I'll just fool him and go back to the barn.

We've had our battles. Duffy has dug up my tulip bulbs outside and upset several houseplants inside. Each time I threaten to kill him. He runs for cover until the storm is over and then he's back, wagging his tail and being the perfect, obedient dog.

Dog hair in every room and in the car is a reality I hate, but I have learned to live with it. What choice do I have?

Unless you want Duffy for company, never jingle your car keys at our house. If there is a chance that we are going anywhere in the car, he's sure he should go too. When he was that small lap-dog size, we usually took him with us in the car and it seems anything we taught him in that first six months of his life he just never forgets.

Longer vacation trips mean I have to either consider a kennel or a sitter. Then I do ask myself if retired people should have pets. I know life might be simpler without him, but where else would I find such good and loyal company that never talks back? Clearly, Duffy doesn't measure up to the dream I had of a *lap* dog, but if you reverse those letters, he is definitely a *pal*.

Dear Hearts and Gentle People

The Tale of Lorraine

Husband Frank loves dogs. Throughout our marriage he has brought home more than one dog or pup. Perhaps the most memorable is the black lab, a beautiful looking dog but far too big for a housedog, or so I thought. The secretary at Frank's office had brought the dog to work one summer day, hoping one of the staff would give it a home. She must have known Frank's weakness for dogs.

Frank could tell by my skeptical look that I was not too impressed with this surprise. I had never been consulted. Frank and the dog just arrived at the door together.

"What's his name?" I asked.

"It's a female and her name is Lorraine."

I tried not to smile. My second name is Lorraine and I'm sure Frank attached this name to the dog at that very opportune moment.

"A female dog. That can only mean trouble," I retorted, trying not to acknowledge any kinship because of the name-game. "She's too big to be in the house."

" We'll keep her tied outside. I'll build her a house."

"Well, she's your responsibility," I said lamely, wishing Lorraine had been a cute, cuddly kitten.

And so, life with Lorraine began on a sour note. The melody didn't get any better either when Frank and I realized that our new neighbour's name was Lorraine. Just try to imagine the reaction of this lady the first time she heard Frank's chorus of, "Lorraine, you come here. Lorraine, I said to come here. Get into that house! Are you demented! Lorraine, do you hear me?"

And as summer turned to fall, and fall to winter, Lorraine remained in our back yard. Well, she was there most of the time. Occasionally she broke free, toured the neighbourhood, tore up other people's garbage, learned to fear a broom, and just made a general nuisance of herself.

Generally she was a very quiet dog. Most Labradors are. But one cold, winter evening, we heard her yelping in the back yard, followed by whining and whimpering and then some more yelping. Frank grabbed the flashlight and went to the back yard to investigate. He was gone for a short while, long enough that I started to the door to look for him only to be met by him hurrying in, his outstretched hands cupped in front of his chest. It was then that I realized that he was carrying five very small, wriggling, newly born puppies. For a minute I just stood in awe. None of us had even realized that Lorraine, really still a pup herself, was pregnant. My maternal instinct took over, especially as it was so cold outside. Poor Lorraine had given birth by herself somewhere out there, and had tried to shelter the puppies in the straw in her cold doghouse.

"We'd better bring her in," I said. "Is this it, or are there more puppies out there?"

Frank took his time in replying. "There are more," he said, "but, ... I am afraid they are pupsicles."

Needless to say, I was a mass of guilt. Lorraine and her family were moved into the house for the winter and we mostly enjoyed, but sometimes only endured the usual tricks associated with new puppies. By spring I had found them all loving homes and that helped somewhat to unload the guilt I had felt because of the "pupsicles". Lorraine eventually endeared herself to a farmer, and I like to think that now she has plenty of room to roam. If she does become a mother again, at least she will hopefully have the benefit of a stable and the warmth of other animals.

As for Frank bringing home any more stray dogs, the experience with Lorraine seems to have been enough to last a lifetime.

Musically Inclined

Dear Hearts and Gentle People

Losing My Bite Over Elvis

It was the summer of 1957. I was seventeen and crazy over Elvis. In fact, every girl I knew sighed when the name Elvis Presley was mentioned. Many young men had adopted the Elvis-style haircut. The hair from the sides of the head was swept up to meet on top of the head, and any curl they could manage was brought forward and resting on the center of the forehead. I thought the style well-suited boyfriend Frank who also had the luck to have black wavy hair just like Elvis.

Elvis had advanced from singing at gigs to starring in movies. For a shy, country boy, he was a pretty good actor, but when he sang who cared whether he could act or not. His song "Love Me Tender", sung to the tune of Aura Lee, was one of my favourites. Now the movie by the same name was coming to the theatre at Bancroft, and I just had to go. Frank, at eighteen, had a car, and was picking me up at seven for the thirty- minute drive to Bancroft.

This was also the days of saddle shoes. Some of you will remember those. The saddle effect was across the instep in a contrasting colour. My shoes were white with a blue and red saddle and white laces. Believe it or not, we teenagers bought bottles of white shoe polish and prided ourselves on having shoes that looked new. My, how times have changed! Well, of course, I had to polish my shoes for this big date, and, clumsy me, I spilled the white polish. What a mess! I was glad most of it was on the newspapers I had put down. Frank was already at the door, but Mom insisted I clean up my mess. Finally, with shoes pearly white and the newspapers in the garbage, we left to make the drive to the theatre.

Just at the edge of Coe Hill is the Deer River and, at that time, the road crossed over it by means of a corner-angled bridge. It was a bad bit of road designing. The bridge was narrow and the angle caused a blind spot for approaching motorists.

We had just entered the bridge when all of a sudden there was a car coming at us and we had no place to go! The bridge had tall cement sides and once you were on it you had no choice. I remember very briefly seeing the car and then not much after that. People living nearby said they heard my screams as well as the crash. I do remember taking my hand away from my mouth and seeing my two front teeth lying in my hand. I must have passed out because the next thing I remember was being on the couch in my parents' home, feeling very cold, and repeating over and over "He's on our hood." Mom wrapped me in a blanket and I heard her say, "I shouldn't have made you clean up the polish." Since Frank had stayed at the accident scene and wasn't with me, poor Mom and Dad thought it was him on our hood. No, I was referring to the other car, but in my state of shock I didn't make a lot of sense.

I was quite a sight for months afterwards. Two more of my front teeth had to be extracted, and to make matters worse, our Bancroft dentist, Doctor Rouse, did not have false teeth in stock that were white enough to match mine and they had to be ordered from Florida. Why, I don't know. In 1957 these things took time. It was weeks before they arrived and then an impression had to be taken of my mouth and a partial plate made to which the four teeth were attached. In the meantime, I had to start grade eleven that year missing four front teeth! I spent most of my time covering my mouth and trying not to laugh. It was embarrassing, to say the least. Eating presented some problems too. In fact, biting into an apple or a cob of corn has never been the same since that accident.

I know I had much to be grateful for. Doctor Rouse said that having my mouth open in a scream when I "bit the dash" was a blessing. Otherwise I would have probably ended up with a split lip and scars. The fact that no one was killed in the accident was, indeed, a big blessing. At seventeen though, I didn't give this as much focus as I do now. No, my main regret at the time was that I had missed seeing Elvis in his famous movie "Love Me Tender", and that it would probably be a long time before I would ever have that chance again.

Dear Hearts and Gentle People

Mr. Wallace's Surprise Symphony

Our high school vocal music teacher, Mr. Wallace, loved his music. He was young enough that he formed close friendships with his pupils, some which continued even after graduation. It was then that many of us called him by his first name, George.

Single, and sporting a white convertible with a red interior, he might have spent his weekend time attracting young women. And George did have dates, but for many years no serious relationships were formed between him and any of these dates.

Some of the best musical presentations took place in Toronto on the weekends. That was a four-hour drive from our area. Often George did not feel up to fighting the traffic on his own so he usually invited Frank to be his chauffeur, or to at least share the driving. Frank looked upon this as a real treat. He was nineteen at the time and no longer in school, but had been one of George's pupils. A family friendship had been formed and George often visited at the Campbell farm.

Frank's favourite memory of George's trips to Toronto is the one taken to Convocation Hall to attend a concert directed by Doctor Fenwick, well-known and highly revered by those who appreciated classical music.

George took Beth, his chosen girl at that time, with him and they chatted amiably all the way to Toronto. The three of them had excellent seats in row three directly in front of the stage. The concert was superb and George resonated with each rendition. Sometimes he would tilt his face heavenward, close his eyes and, whether it was Chopin, Mozart, or Beethoven, seem to be inhaling the symphonies. The finale, unfortunately, came too soon. The crowd rose at the end in applause and appreciation, none more appreciative than George.

Then the houselights came on and people funneled out, hailing taxis or heading for the parking lot. Frank was a few steps ahead of George and kept his eye trained on the exit door. In the dark outside he turned around long enough to say, "The car is parked at the end of this row, George." Then off he went to lead the way.

Frank unlocked his door and George's as he settled beneath the wheel. George, arriving a few steps behind, opened his door exclaiming, "Wasn't that wonderful! Doctor Fenwick lent so much of himself to that music. Are you feeling up to driving the first shift?"

"Yes, but where is Beth?"

"Oh my gosh!" George gasped, looking at Frank in disbelief. "I'd better go back and find her."

Like I said, for some reason, at that time, no serious relationships had ever formed between George and any of his dates!

A Special Gift

"I fell down on the ice with this on my way to the bus this morning. I hope it's not broken," my boyfriend, Frank, said as he handed me my Christmas gift. I noticed at once that it was wrapped in very dark green, crepe paper rather than the traditional tissue gift-wrap, but I smiled and took it from him. We were each grade eleven students and this was his very first Christmas gift to me, or gift of any kind for that matter.

"I never open my gifts before Christmas, but if you really want me to, I guess I could." I added the last few words in response to the crestfallen look on his face.

"Well, if it's broken I'd like to know."

"O.K., but let's not do it here in the hallway," I said, shutting my locker door. "Maybe there's an empty classroom. I don't want everyone staring."

The two of us tried to appear nonchalant as we peeked into nearby classrooms, finally finding the music room empty. "This is appropriate, isn't it? The room where we met." That had been two years ago when I had been smitten by Frank's good looks and charm and had welcomed the chance to share a desk. Over those two years we had continued to have our music class together. Not only had we learned about music, but also we had learned about each other. We had visited at each other's homes and became acquainted with each other's family. I knew that his family struggled financially but were well-respected in the community. Farming had never provided much of an income and so now they had only their own garden and some apple trees. Through the summer, Frank worked long, twelve-hour shifts in a sawmill. The salary earned there was his spending money for the entire year. I knew that some of it had purchased this gift.

We left the door of the music room open, but took the gift to a table at the back of the room. Untying the ribbon and pulling off the green, heavy paper, I took the lid off the cardboard box inside. Then very carefully I lifted out a beautiful, black lacquered box trimmed with pink and white mother of pearl. "A jewellery box!" I exclaimed and opened the lid. As I did, a few musical notes tinkled and then quit. "Oh, should it play a tune?" I ventured.

" I sure hope so. When I fell, the parcel flew out of my hand, slid along the ice and played a great tune, not that I really appreciated it right then. I hope that all it needs is to be wound again."

He shut the lid, turned the box over, and gave the key on the bottom a few turns. Then he handed it back to me. "See what happens now."

Cautiously I raised the lid. At once the two diminutive ballerina figurines inside started to twirl and I recognized the melody that was playing. It was *The Anniversary Waltz* . Frank and I had gone to the theatre earlier in the year to see "The Al Jolson Story" and I had been awed by actor Larry Park's singing of that song. Little did I know that it was to become "our song".

The ugly green crepe paper was soon forgotten as I marveled at the treasure that it had concealed. Forty-four years have passed since that day. Frank and I have been married for forty-one of those years, continuing to share our love of singing and making music. Over the years there have been countless other gifts, most costing much more than this music box and wrapped in the best of papers. Each in turn has been much appreciated, but none will quite measure up to that first gift. That music box still occupies a special spot; not only is it proudly displayed in our bedroom, but the memory of receiving it is locked forever in my heart.

Heather Campbell

A Memorable Funeral

As the local church's supply organist, I had been booked for the summer months' services, including appointed weddings and, by chance, any funerals. My third week on the job and it happened, the death of one of the parishioners. I knew it would be a large funeral because the deceased had been a delightful, fun-filled, well-loved lady, and from a large family.

Remembering the lengthy prelude time for a previous funeral for which I had played, I dutifully set about preparing an abundance of organ music. I felt quite proud of the three different medleys of appropriate music I had arranged. Having timed myself as I practised, I knew that I could play for at least twenty minutes before I would need to consider repeating any of the music.

On the day of the funeral, with great confidence, twenty minutes before the scheduled service time I started my prelude organ music. My back being to the congregation, I now and then stole a glance in the rear-view mirrors that are mounted on the organ and trained on the church's front doors. Anytime now I expected to see the undertaker, the pallbearers, the casket, and the immediate family arriving. Anxiously I periodically checked my watch. The appointed hour came and went and still no casket, no corpse, and not even any of the immediate family had arrived. By now the choir had filed into the choir loft in front of me. They too were exchanging puzzled and somewhat perturbed glances. Our minister entered from her office and indicated to me with shrugged shoulders, upturned palms, and a brave little smile that she had not heard any news. It would be unheard of to begin a funeral without the body and the family!

I wondered how many more times this congregation could accept my repeated renditions. Although it was now twenty minutes past the hour and I was starting my medleys for the third time, I was almost positive this funeral would at some point begin. A person could change their mind about a wedding, but a funeral is a pretty sure and final destination!

I could hear whispers and even mumbled voices, each one expounding their theory on the absent corpse. Another five minutes ticked by. Still no phone call nor runner. I had now been playing for forty-five minutes. The choir director began handing me new music and suggestions for different pieces. In spite of the respect entitled the departed, we were all stifling the odd snicker. There is certainly truth in the old adage "Better to laugh than cry". Five or six more anxious minutes lapsed. Then we heard voices and the sound of people arriving. To our relief the doors swung open to reveal the casket ready to be rolled down the aisle. I felt like swinging into a rendition of *Hail, Hail the Gang's All Here*! But I guess the *Jesus, We Just Want to Thank You* that I was playing suited the moment anyway!

    The minister, who had been quickly briefed, offered the funeral home's apology. The hearse had broken down midway on the fifteen-mile trip and a second one had to be summoned and the casket transferred. No one from the funeral home had thought to bring a cell phone, and in the confusion no one tried to call us from a nearby house.

    As a calm descended on the weary congregation and the casket was ceremoniously ushered to the front of the church, I was sure I heard a muffled little giggle. I bet this was one time the corpse definitely had a smile on her face!

Bathroom Banter

Birthday Excitement

My aunt and uncle's house had a unique bathroom door. The key was on the inside of the door. By that I mean you went in through the door, closed it, and then to lock the door you turned a regular type key which was usually left right in the key hole. I expect it was really an outside door that had been converted to be used indoors.

Anyway, it worked out fine until my Aunt Mary had a birthday party for her youngest daughter. Eventually one of the little girlfriends attending the party had to use the bathroom. Upstairs she went, all on her own, and nothing more was heard from her for a long time. Of course it was very noisy downstairs with all the shrieking from the game of "pin the tail on the donkey". Finally that game was over and my aunt was herding the children to the table when shrieking from another source was heard. Everybody stopped and listened intently.

"Mary, I can't get out, I can't get out!"

Aunt Mary went upstairs to investigate, followed by all the little guests.

"Janet, are you in there?" Aunt Mary called from outside the bathroom door.

"Yes, " she sobbed. "The door won't open."

"You have to turn the key."

"I did."

"Well do it again."

"I'm scared."

Then more wailing and sobbing came, not only from within, but also from without because, by now, other little guests were upset over Janet being locked in the bathroom.

There's not much point trying to reason with a four-year old trapped in the bathroom. There had to be another solution. Aunt Mary looked at her own daughter who, although she was seven years old, was very tiny. A plan was hatching!

"Lois, I'm going to put a ladder up to the woodshed roof. You can get onto the roof and from there you'll be able to get to the bathroom window. I think it's open a bit. You can push it up enough to climb in and then unlock the door.

The fearless seven-year old climbed up gingerly while the adult moms stood below with hearts pounding, watching Lois's every move. Occasionally there would be a "Good girl, Lois" or "Be careful, don't fall" from the anxious team of coaches huddled outside.

Inside the house, Janet's older sister, Brenda, stood outside the bathroom door pleading with Janet to stop crying and assuring her that Lois was going to come in the window and get the door open. Janet continued to sob.

Finally the daring rescue took place, the bathroom door was flung open, and Janet, followed by Lois, came bolting out and into the arms of relieved sisters and moms.

Lois was the hero of the day for sure. Later the traditional birthday cake and ice cream were served, after which all the guests left happily. Needless to say, it was a birthday party remembered for years to come, especially by Janet Mawdsley.

My "Locked Up" Experiences

A bathroom, in our civilized lifestyles, is a necessity of life. In my life this necessity has twice become a prison.

The first prison sentence was given in the first year of our marriage. We lived in an upstairs apartment in a small building that had only three other apartments. The apartment consisted of a bedroom and a combined kitchen-living room. It was so small that we used to joke about how you could sit on the sofa and put your feet in the sink! But it was cheap, close to my work, and the two of us were together there only on weekends. Frank's work took him out of town through the week.

Notice I have not mentioned anything about the bathroom being part of the apartment. That's because it wasn't. It was a separate room, without its own source of heat, located across the hall. Why this arrangement, I don't know. I assume that the building had not really been originally designed as an apartment building.

One February weekend Frank decided that he would go into Oshawa, our nearest city, to make a purchase. I chose to stay

Dear Hearts and Gentle People

behind and get some work done. As nature would have it, I soon was called to the bathroom. I shivered as I hurried across the hall and into the frigid bathroom. I made my business time there as short as possible and hurried out. Grabbing the doorknob of the apartment, I tried to open the door but the knob resisted. I tried again and again but no luck. For some reason, out of pure habit I guess, I had locked the door when I left. I had neither key nor coat. I knew the landlord wasn't at home. We had lived there only a month and I did not know the other occupants and they wouldn't have had a key anyway. We were urban dwellers then, not enjoying the rural, friendly environment that we now know. I was still in my housecoat, really not dressed for visiting with perfect strangers. I knew that Frank would be gone at least an hour. Sitting down and waiting was the only solution and the only seat available was in the bathroom. So there I sat, not even a book to read. For thirty minutes I alternated between meditating, singing quietly, crying quietly, and praying. God must have heard my prayers because I heard Frank's footsteps on the stairs much sooner than I had expected. Was I glad to see him!

From that day on, no matter in what house we have lived, there has always been reading material in the bathroom. In fact, I try to keep pencil and paper there too. You never know when you might have an experience worth writing about!

❧❧❧❧❧❧❧❧❧❧❧❧❧

I experienced my second bathroom prison rather recently. For many years we had had a cottage lot, but no cottage. We owned a trailer equipped with all the comforts of home and we simply parked that on our lot. But then a few years ago after I retired, we found we were spending more time at the cottage lot. The trailer now seemed too small and cramped. Last year we decided that we would start building a cottage. We just moved the trailer to one side of the lot but continued to live in it while all the digging and building details were taking place. Frank helped with as much of this as possible.

The excavation to make the hole needed for the septic system was very noisy. A local operator had brought his backhoe and he and his hired help and Frank were hard at work. I watched for awhile but decided I had things to do in the trailer. Eventually I felt the need to visit the bathroom. The bathrooms in trailers are very small. In our trailer the bathroom door opened opposite the refrigerator.

When I tried to open the bathroom door to leave, it would not budge. I pushed and pushed but the best I could do was open it just a crack that was wide enough to see that our dog had come into the trailer. I could see him and he could see me but couldn't help me nor explain why the door wouldn't open.

The window in the bathroom was very small. If I knelt on the toilet seat I could see the men working. I slid the glass back and yelled at them. In fact, I screamed but because of the noisy engine no one heard me. The window screen was not removable. Otherwise, I might have started pitching things out the window to see if I could attract their attention. Yes, I normally would have had magazines to read, but there wasn't a spot big enough in this bathroom to stack them. What I did have was a cell phone. For some reason I had had it in my hand and had absent-mindedly taken it into the bathroom. But what good was that when no one outside had a phone and we had no close neighbours? Our cottage is in the wilds. So I waited, pushed on the door some more, screamed some more, and just generally cussed myself for getting into this predicament. Almost forty years had passed since my first bathroom prison experience and here I was incarcerated again! At least this time it was warm. I knew that it could be a very long time before the men would stop work. Would Frank wonder where I was or what I was doing? Probably not, not until he was hungry anyway.

Time dragged on. The cell phone was my only link with the world. Maybe my daughter would like to come for a visit. Why hadn't I thought of this before? She was only thirty minutes away. I picked up the phone and punched in her number. Although I had to strain to hear over the noise of the backhoe, it was good to talk to her. She was most sympathetic about my situation but had an appointment to keep and couldn't come. She'd check with me again when she got home!

More time ticked by and more futile screaming out the window. Then the phone rang. It was my mother who lives in a seniors' home. "Why is it so noisy there?" she asked. I told her my predicament. Again, I received sincere sympathy but no solution. I must admit though, it was comforting to talk to someone.

Just when I was thinking of others I could call, I heard the engine change from a roar to a purring sound. I scrambled up to window level again and screamed Frank's name. This time I was noticed. Frank started my way to investigate while I kept screaming, "I'm in the bathroom. The door won't open!"

Soon I heard him on the other side telling the dog to get out of the way. Then I heard the fridge door being slammed shut. At that point I gave a slight push on the bathroom door and presto! It opened without any problem.

I guess I had left the fridge door ajar and the dog must have caught it with his wagging tail, sending it bumping up against the bathroom door and wedging itself there. Had our trailer been level, this probably would not have happened. We had not bothered to level it up in our hurried moving. With all the noise outside I had not noticed the bumping sound the door must have made as it lodged itself against the bathroom. Even if I had, the result would have been the same. No amount of pushing from my side would have moved that wedge. I hate to imagine the panic I would have been in had I been all alone the day this happened.

Perhaps I'd be wise to carry some reading material, maybe even a cell phone, to any bathroom I enter. It seems history does repeat itself!

The Interment

In the 1940's, we in rural Ontario were all very familiar with the outhouse. Some people referred to it as the *privy*, the *outdoor john*, or the *outdoor toilet*. No matter what you labeled them, they were all pretty much the same. Each was about four feet by four feet with a raised bench in which a hole had been cut, or sometimes two holes so that you and a buddy could do your "business" at the same time. This particular structure was appropriately known as a "two-holer". Underneath this building was a deep pit that some family member had to dig before the building was set on the site. Eventually this pit would get pretty full of all that "good stuff", and then it was time to get some strong muscles to dig a new pit and move the privy.

Some people painted the inside of the toilet. Others just let the boards weather. But, painted or not, it was the custom to cut out choice, colourful pictures from magazines and tack them on the walls. After all, if you had to sit there for awhile, you might as well have pleasant surroundings.

A cousin of my husband's, whom I will call Earl, was about three years old and just getting to the stage of real independence. His favourite words were, "No, I can do it myself." And so he was allowed to go to the outdoor privy on his own. A little stepstool had been set up to make his ascent to the "throne" a bit easier.

One day when Earl visited this throne by himself, he was gone for a very long time. His Mom, whom we will call Nora, thought she'd better check on him. Off she went to the backyard privy. As she approached she heard some shrieking and a lot of thumping coming from inside. With her heart pounding, she quickened her step. What Nora had most dreaded had happened! Earl was not sitting on the throne. He was, so to speak, under the throne! Now that his Mom was on the scene, he sobbed hysterically from the mess below. Nora screamed for Earl's brother to go and get the doctor who was vacationing in a nearby cottage. By the time Nora had Earl hauled out of the awful pit, the doctor had arrived. Then Nora broke into tears. Earl was strangely quiet and Nora feared he had suffered permanent damage.

"Let me examine him. You go back to the house and get him some clean clothes, and some soapy water," advised the doctor.

When Nora returned she was pleased to see the doctor smiling. "Well, Nora, Earl's not dead, but he is *in turd*!"

Never had a pun been so appropriate! In spite of Earl's helpless state, Nora convulsed in laughter. When Earl saw his mother laughing, he laughed too. Somehow after that, the clean-up was so much easier. It's a wise doctor who knows that laughter is the best medicine!

Life's Little Challenges

Dear Hearts and Gentle People

Looking Gift Horses in the Mouth

When is a deal not a deal? Would it be fair to say "most of the time"?

Several years ago I had experiences with "gift horses". I was shopping in a department store and feeling particularly benevolent. I have great respect for university students who work to make extra money. I was easily convinced by a mannerly young student that I should apply for the store's credit card. In return for just filling out the application, I would be given a gold-plated chain. In addition, I would receive a ten percent discount on my total purchases the first time that I used the card.

True to his word, the young man handed me the chain as soon as the application was completed. In about three weeks I received the credit card and a reminder about the ten percent discount.

I pride myself on my ability to handle money and so I did not immediately rush out to buy something frivolous. I had told myself that I would wait until I needed something. Months passed until one day, on examining the card, I noticed that I had to use the card within the calendar year in order to take advantage of the discount. Being both a busy person and a forgetful one, I thought I'd better act soon or I would lose out. I did need a mat to go in front of the kitchen sink and there was an anniversary present that I should buy too.

I drove the distance to that particular store, one where I seldom shop because it is too far away, telling myself that the discount made it all worthwhile. While traveling the aisles to find the mats, I couldn't help but notice that the winter clothing had all been substantially reduced. I really wasn't in need of anything, but I have two granddaughters. Even though I already had their Christmas gifts bought and wrapped, I decided to buy one or two of these sale items and put them away for birthday gifts. I'd be saving even more because of my ten percent discount. After all, I might as well make my trip count, I reasoned.

The mat and the anniversary gift totalled fifty-five dollars. The grand total of my bill was one hundred and fifty-one dollars. I had spent ninety- six dollars more than I needed, but look at the savings!

About two months later the gift horse whinnied again. In the mail I received a coupon offering me a free set of elegant tumblers. All I had to do was make a ten-dollar purchase using the same card again. I carried the coupon in my purse for a week but by then it had eaten the proverbial hole. My daughter needed more tumblers, I reasoned, and I wanted to buy my two young granddaughters each an Easter hat.

Off I went to that distant store again. Once again, there were sale signs everywhere. This time my bill totaled over seventy-five dollars. The prize tumblers turned out to be a set of four. Although they are good quality tumblers, I asked myself if they were really free. How much of that seventy-five dollars worth of purchases did I really need right now?

As embarrassed as I am to admit it, this store had no Easter hats. I still ended up going to another store to buy these. Incidentally, that is all I bought there. I had no coupons to tempt me!

Years have passed but not temptations. Right now I am staring at a flyer that is offering me two times the amount of cash bonus coupons if I shop on a certain day. Will I accept this gift horse?

I don't think so. Over the years I figure I have paid plenty for gold chains, tumblers, and a host of other "free" trinkets. It's definitely time to have that horse's mouth checked!

Hiding Your Skates in a Stump

"I'm hiding my skates in a stump," I said to Frank, placing the container of muffins between the car seats as we arrived at our friends' house. They had invited us on short notice for dessert and coffee. Frank nodded knowingly. That phrase at our house is what we call an "in-joke". Only the family members understand. Let me fill you in:

Frank's family lived about two miles out of the village of

Lake St. Peter, Ontario. Their farm was on a wooded, winding road, with two pretty steep hills enroute. You passed only three or four other houses on that two-mile stretch, all well separated from one another. For most of Frank's growing-up years, the farmhouse had no telephone. What was happening down in the village remained a mystery until he arrived. For many years he arrived either in the wagon pulled by a team of horses, or he walked.

Frank loved to play hockey and at that time, outdoor rinks were the norm. That meant that snowstorms led to shoveling off the rink. With Frank so far from the community, he had no idea as to whether any of his friends were skating, shoveling, or already playing a makeshift game of hockey. He hated to be seen with his skates over his shoulder if no one else his age was going to be on the rink. That would be something like wearing your snow boots in the middle of summer, or having mismatched socks! How embarrassing, especially once you reached those teen years!

Nature had provided an old hollowed out stump about a quarter mile from the village and well hidden by other trees. Frank would walk from his house, carrying his skates and hoping his friends would be skating, but to save face, he would put his skates in this stump and continue down the road to where he could see the rink. If his friends were there he hurried back, yanked his skates from the stump, flung them over his shoulder, and arrived nonchalantly at the rink, ready for action!

As for my muffins, they stayed "in the stump". The rest of the desserts looked too good and I didn't want to embarrass myself with contributing plain old muffins. Just like the skates on a non-skating day, I carted them home again with no one being the wiser!

Purse-Packing Predicament

I sometimes wonder what women did before the invention of the purse. I doubt that it was a man who came up with the idea of a purse because very few North American men even today have adopted the idea.

Most ladies' purses equal a small suitcase. Although a few

of us carry the same purse all year, most women change with the seasons, sporting a dark colour bag for winter and a light colour for summer. Of course, we all have those smaller, dainty purses referred to as evening bags that we bring out for "dress occasions". They are designed for only the bare necessities. Mine is usually packed to the bulging point. Granted, I'm noted for doing that with even the largest purse. The bigger it is, the more I pack into it!

Somewhere between my mother's era and mine, manufacturers added a longer strap to the purse and it became a shoulder bag. By the time a girl has reached twenty-five, grabbing that shoulder bag as she leaves the house is an inborn, automatic motion. The essential cosmetics, comb, nail file, tissues, address book, pills, mints, driver's licence, glasses, credit cards, photos, pen, keys and wallet are always packed (How do men manage without purses I wonder!). I even carry a paperback novel in mine so that I can read when I have to wait in line-ups.

We women learned that Boy Scout motto "Always be prepared" without even having to attend scout meetings. With rare exception, our purses are always ready. One of those rare exceptions was the case of a local lady who stopped at the Canadian Diabetic Association's office recently to make a donation. This donation was to be in memory of a deceased friend and a card would be sent to the family. The lady gave the particulars of names and addresses in great detail. She double-checked everything that the clerk had typed to make sure it was correct. Then, still talking, she automatically opened her purse to make the cash donation. Without even looking down, she plunged her hand inside to retrieve her wallet. As her hand did a complete slide to the bottom of the lining, she stopped mid-sentence and opened the purse wider. What an embarrassing moment! The entire contents consisted of a gum wrapper, a lone penny, and a ratty tissue. It was then she remembered that she had bought herself a new purse and just that morning had transferred all the valuable contents from this old one to the new one!

There is something universal about how comfortable we become with shoes and purses. Even though this lady had opened up her new purse to get her keys only minutes before she left the house, she still grabbed the old purse as she departed. I guess the only solution to this foible is to make sure we introduce any worn out purse to the garbage as soon as we make the content transfer.

As for having a purse to match the season, maybe we need someone to come up with an all-seasons purse; just unzip the outer covering and a new colour is underneath. Well, all you designers, I've planted the seed, you take it from there!

Cookie Stress

I enjoy teaching, writing, piano playing, crocheting, reading, gardening, and a host of other things, - in fact, almost anything that doesn't involve hours spent in the kitchen!

Oh yes, I have tried to be the answer to the domestic "wonderwoman" at our house. When you have a family you usually don't have much choice. Preparing the main course for a meal is not a problem; in fact I love the creativity it allows. In contrast, following a baking recipe that has a precise, expected outcome is a challenge. I think my family would give me an E for effort when it comes to baking, but they must know I struggle.

One of my biggest domestic challenges is making cookies. I enjoy eating them, but not making them. I justify that by saying that it's the same as a person who loves to read a story but not write it, or a person who loves a crocheted sweater but would never dream of making one.

The cookies that I most enjoy lately are those cookies that are stored in files in my computer. There again though, I know nothing about how they are made, just that they are part of the computer that I have grown to love so much.

Then there are the cookies we use to play crokinole, and those have been popular with me since childhood. I love a game of good old-fashioned crokinole where you can jet propel those little wooden cookies and blast your opponent into the gutter, all in good fun, of course. What great therapy for relieving stress!

On the other hand, being in the kitchen with a cookie recipe in front of me has often been a sress-inducer. I'm certainly not like my Grandma who seldom had a written recipe, but knew by the look and the feel of the dough how much more flour or sugar or liquid was needed. All her cookies were so uniform in size and became golden-brown beauties that melted in your mouth. I wish I'd stayed in her kitchen and learned from her. I know for sure my family will never remember me for the cookies I make!

Cookies, especially, have so much traditional attachment. Serving cookies and tea has been an expected thing when visitors drop by. Taking cookies to a sick friend is as good as taking flowers, maybe better. Cookies are a favourite part of Christmas baking. Now that it is November, the fancy storage containers at our house sit waiting. Will I be filling them again this year with the home baking that I buy?

Believe me, I have attempted to fit the mold. Early in our marriage we bought a house in the city. For a while I was the "new kid" on the block and was much younger than my neighbours, and lonely. Then a young couple moved into the house behind us. Her name was Heather, the same as mine, and I was so anxious to become good friends and to make her feel welcome. With my country background, I naturally thought of welcoming her with home baking. I'd make some cookies! And so I did. Oatmeal cookies that, once in the oven, spread out about three times the size I intended, and became far too brown. I had spent the best part of the afternoon making these cookies and then cleaning up the resulting kitchen mess. I did the taste-test and told myself they were pretty good. I picked out the best ten or twelve, put them on a plate and crossed the back yard to my new neighbour.

Heather greeted me at the door and I mumbled something about a welcoming gift and handed her my offering. Forty years later I can still remember her amused expression as she looked at my creations. I think she did say thank-you but she never invited me in and I never heard another word about those cookies or the thought behind them. After all, isn't it supposed to be the thought that counts? No, we didn't become the friends that I had dreamed of, and I think this whole experience coloured my cookie-making world forever.

I have recognized finally that I am definitely baking-challenged and should stick to making casseroles and squares, the standard menu at our house. However, if you meet my children or my husband anywhere and you're one of those talented, at-home-in-the-kitchen ladies that I admire, please take pity and offer them a cookie!

Dear Hearts and Gentle People

Whoa is Woe

Perhaps the most amusing tale I've ever heard about my Grandfather Henry Gunter was left out of my first book. The reason was that I heard the story from cousin, Ivan Gunter, after the book was published. Here it is as I remember Ivan telling it:

▲▲▲▲▲▲▲▲▲▲▲▲

Grandpa Henry had bought a car for his sons Roscoe and Howard (my dad). It was in the late 1920's and the car was starting to replace the horse and buggy as the means of transportation. Roscoe and Howard both knew how to drive but Henry didn't. Why is it that young people take to any new technology so readily but the older generation is in awe of it all?

Grandpa Henry, like most of the "old-timers", rather than hitching up the horses, stabling them in town, and then tending to them again on returning home, would simply walk the two and one-half miles to and from town. Roscoe and Howard thought it only right though that their dad should learn to drive and they proceeded to teach him. Henry wasn't too sure that he wanted to learn but he went along with his coaches. The two brothers thought their dad was doing pretty well and left him on his own at the wheel. He toured around the farm rather proud of his accomplishments. Finally he drove the car into the barn at the top of the hill. Roscoe and Howard were within earshot and they soon heard their father yelling, "Whoa, whoa, whoa!" with each "whoa" being louder than the one before.

The boys surmised the problem right away and started yelling, "Put the brake on, Dad! Put the brake on!"

Their instructions seemed lost on the wind. The car, with Henry at the wheel, came bursting out the other end of the barn and Henry was still commanding it to "Whoa, whoa!"

By now, Howard and Roscoe were in fits of laughter but tried to run a little closer, all the time yelling, "Push the brake pedal, Dad, the brake, the brake!"

Meanwhile Henry and car careened down the hill, across the bumpy field, and finally lurched to a stop in the field of stubble.

Grandpa opened the car door, got out, slammed it with a vengeance, glared in the direction of his sons, and stomped away. He had had his fill of "the iron horse". That was the last time that he ever got behind the wheel of a car. He stuck to what he knew best, even if it did require feed, water, and an occasional rubdown!

Howard with the car that would not whoa!

Believe It or Not

Uncle Ab's Story

When you've been raised in the country and kept a garden, it's hard to leave that gardening fever behind even though you move to the city. That was the case with Frank's Uncle Ab Carswell and his wife, Eva. Uncle Ab had been raised in Maynooth, and Aunt Eva was the former Eva Card from Lake St. Peter, Ontario. For most of their married lives, however, they lived in Oshawa where Uncle Ab was a worker at General Motors. Frank loves to tell a favourite tale of his uncle's.

True to their country roots, Ab and Eva grew a small but much-prized garden behind their house in Oshawa. Good fertilizer was important. There was nothing better than farm manure, especially for the strawberry plants, and so Uncle Ab used to go to the farm at the mental institution at nearby Whitby. One time while shoveling his load of manure into a wheelbarrow, he overheard one of the newer patients ask another, "What is that guy doing?"

"He's getting manure to take home."

"Why?"

"He takes it home and puts it on his strawberries."

The new patient shook his head. "Boy, he's sure stupid. Maybe he should be in here with us. At least we know enough to put brown sugar on our berries!"

Getting to the Root of It

In 1991 we had a new dentist in our little town that is about ninety miles from Ottawa. For the sake of all concerned in this tale, I will call him Doctor Ripper. Newspaper reporters in 1994 were less kind.

I was one of the many townsfolk who thought it made sense to take our business to "the local fellow" instead of making a twenty-minute drive to our usual dentist. Doctor Ripper was extremely good looking, had a practice in Ottawa as well, and was very friendly and quite charming. The initial visits in his early months went well. In fact things went so well that I consented to a root canal treatment for an ailing tooth. I never thought to get a second opinion, so confident was I that Dr. Ripper knew his business. At the time I noticed that he worked without rubber gloves and his hands reeked of tobacco smoke, but I dismissed any misgivings I had with the thought that perhaps I was just too particular.

Then in July of 1992, I received a letter from Revenue Canada saying that any future fees owed to Doctor Ripper should be sent to Revenue Canada. The letter indicated that the doctor owed Revenue Canada a six-digit sum. Of course when I showed this to Dr.Ripper at my next appointment, he claimed it was an error and that I should ignore it.

By then I had been talking to other patients who were concerned because the doctor always wanted his money first before he did the work. Others were tired of having appointments continually cancelled supposedly because supplies had been delayed, or the wrong material sent, or he was delayed by unexpected emergencies in Ottawa. I had also heard that the Medical Centre that was renting Doctor Ripper the office space was having difficulty collecting the rent. Another source told me that Doctor Ripper's dental assistant was also upset by the shortcuts he took in procedures and she had noticed that he constantly changed suppliers because he was refused deliveries unless his bill was paid. After six months she found work elsewhere and Doctor Ripper tried to manage on his own.

I no longer felt comfortable having this man working on my teeth. His charm had tarnished. I was too embarrassed to return to my old dentist, but fortunately I was able to find another dentist accepting new patients. That was a good thing because by the fall of 1992, I was experiencing jolting discomfort in the area of my root canal treatment. My new dentist referred me to an endodontist in Ottawa. What a revelation that brought!

My tooth had ulcerated. Why? Because the root canal had not been cleaned out properly. I guess Dr. Ripper had used one of his shortcuts. What's more, there was a piece of metal lodged in this whole mess, thanks to an instrument that had broken off while Dr.Ripper had been doing this root canal treatment. Doctor Ripper had never mentioned this. The medical terminology was: *This previous root canal treatment was judged to be inadequate with what ap-*

peared to be a separated instrument in the mesial root and periapical inflammatory areas showing on the radiograph. The endodontist tried to dislodge the metal from the outside but failed. I was booked for surgery to either remove the metal or seal it in so that the root canal could be properly treated. About seven hundred dollars later, this was accomplished. I was glad the dentist was able to retrieve the piece of metal because I was not anxious to have it as a permanent sealed-in feature. I was also happy that my tooth had not been sacrificed.

A friend of mine was not so lucky. A victim of Dr. Ripper's inadequate root canal procedures, she eventually had to have the one tooth pulled.

Another friend had consented to having all her teeth pulled, thinking it would be cheaper than root canals. Dr. Ripper did the extractions right in his office in three separate appointments and each was a harrowing experience from which she emerged black and blue. In response to her screaming, Doctor Ripper told her that she didn't know the difference between pressure and pain. Both sets of dentures that he made were so uncomfortable she couldn't wear them. She has had a new pair made by a different dentist but has had to pay for them herself since her insurance would not cover a second set.

Shortly after these alarming experiences, we heard rumours that a few years earlier Doctor Ripper had been convicted of trafficking in cocaine. Was this the cause of his problems we wondered?

Finally, each of us in turn, reported Doctor Ripper to the Royal College of Dental Surgeons, and two of us obtained lawyers. Doctor Ripper waived his right of appeal. His licence to practise in Ontario was revoked. Had he appealed, he could have continued practising for a year while awaiting the outcome! Obviously he had played this game before. He did not panic, but simply moved himself to a new province. Word has it that he is teaching at a dental college there. What a scary thought!

My advice: If you have a good dentist, don't go looking for a new one, no matter what the distance. The old adage "Beware of wolves in sheep's clothing" is still worth heeding.

Campbell Duplication

Two people having the same last name and each being teachers and from the same small village can cause endless duplication dilemmas.

Jackie Campbell, who is no relation to me, and I have learned to be very careful before ripping open the letters received in the mail. Too many times we realized that the letter was really for the other Mrs. Campbell. You can't really blame the postmistress for not noticing that it was for Mrs. Peter Campbell and not Mrs. Frank, or vice versa.

One time while grocery shopping, Jackie was asked by another shopper as to whether or not she was taking any more students. Jackie thought that was a strange question. A schoolteacher doesn't get the choice of how many students she will take. She tried to tactfully explain this to the woman who had asked.

The woman now seemed perplexed. "You teach piano lessons, don't you?"

Now Jackie understood the problem. Since I retired from regular classroom teaching, I have been teaching piano lessons to a few students. Jackie explained that she didn't even play the piano, but Heather Campbell did. In our minds the two of us don't look alike, but obviously, to some people, we must.

The mail mix-up and the piano student question we laugh about, but when it comes to medical charts or anything concerning money, the anxiety level tends to rise.

Jackie still shakes her head in disbelief over a doctor's appointment she had years ago in nearby Pembroke. Neither of us had lived too long in the area and, unknown to her, I had also visited this same clinic.

Jackie had been having extreme pain in her shoulder, relating to an earlier car accident. She had been for x-rays and now was at the clinic to hear the doctor's verdict. The nurse handed the doctor Jackie's file and Jackie followed him into his inner office. The doctor studied the file for a few minutes and then said, "Really Mrs. Campbell, I don't see anything here that would indicate why your shoulder should be troubling you so much. I see where your neck has given you trouble. How is it now?'

"My neck has never troubled me. It's my shoulder and into my arm. Why wouldn't it give trouble?" Jackie asked in bewilderment. " I'm missing a piece of bone right here," she said, pointing to the top of her shoulder. "My file should have details about the car accident I had three years ago!"

The doctor looked puzzled, flipped through the pages in the file, and scratched his head.

"I had x-rays two weeks ago. Isn't there anything there about it?"

The doctor looked at the name on the file. "Are you Heather Campbell?" he asked.

Jackie groaned and I'm sure she wondered if she would be cursed with being mistaken for me even in her casket. Now doesn't that thought just open up a volume of possibilities!

But the worst has happened since I retired. In fact, Jackie is hoping that any day now she will receive my pension cheques!

Jackie tells me that shortly after I retired her drug benefit card was rendered "void" when she gave it to our local pharmacist to pay for her prescription.

"That's impossible," she said when he told her that her card was invalid. "Why would such a thing happen?"

The pharmacist did some checking and the report came back indicating that this teacher had retired. "I only wish," Jackie sighed.

Finally, a status check was done and the real Jackie Campbell emerged, fully qualified and still employed. The drug card was now recognized as valid and Jackie could breathe freely.

Then two weeks ago it seemed I had invaded her life again. She was in Ottawa with a friend who had paid for tickets to the hockey game. At suppertime Jackie announced that she was paying for the meal and handed the waiter her credit card. The waiter thanked her, disappeared, and then returned to the table and asked if Jackie could come to the desk for a minute. There she explained that their machine was showing that the card's limit had already been reached. Right away Jackie thought of me. Was even the bank confusing us? Had Heather maxed out her card? Fortunately Jackie had another card from a different bank and was relieved that this one gave no problem. She said she did worry as to just what had happened with the first card and, as soon as she arrived home, she checked it by using her on-line banking. All her money was still there and it did not appear that the card had been used by anyone else. There was no mention of my name or any evidence that I was a factor! When she related all this to me I laughed and assured her that, to my knowledge, I still had ample room on my card so I didn't think I was the reason. It does make you wonder though how these things can happen and what little gremlins are lurking in our computers.

Jackie will probably retire in about five years. Already I'm wondering about her first pension cheque. Will we each get a cheque or will the computer kick one of us out?

"Paneless" Punctuality

My husband has always worked in the road engineering field, dating back to the1960's when the government office was called the Department of Highways. He has worked in all kinds of weather and with all kinds of people. He has many fond and entertaining tales of some unique characters.

One tale is of the time he worked in Denbeigh, Ontario, in March of 1960, with a rugged, thirty-year old fellow called Tom Wingle. Tom worked hard and drank hard, the latter getting a real exercising on the weekend. But one thing he prided himself on was never being late for work. No matter what the level of consumption was the night before, Tom was at the job on time the next morning.

March in Ontario can be bitterly cold. On his way to work one Monday morning in his usually reliable Chevrolet, Tom had the misfortune to have the heater motor quit. Any Canadian knows what that means – you have no defrost and it isn't long before your windshield is so frosted over that it's impossible to see a thing. Besides that problem, you become very cold. Well, this was before the days of C.A.A. insurance, and the traffic at six in the morning near Denbeigh is almost non-existent. Tom was in a predicament.

After some peering under the hood, a few unprintable

blessings, and a cigarette or two, Tom opened the car's trunk. What did he find in there to help him? Would you believe a tire iron? I'm sure you're wondering how something used to change a tire could help with a frosted windshield.

Tom went to the front of the vehicle, lifted the iron with both hands and swung! He continued to do this until he had the windshield pane on the driver's side completely smashed out. Being quite warm by then, he pulled his parka snuggly around his head, crawled into his remodeled Chevy and headed for the jobsite. It was quite a sight to see Tom pulling in, shivering in his parka, frost on his eyebrows, and framed by the jagged bits of glass left on the edges of the windshield opening. What did he do on crawling out of his "frostmobile"? He checked his watch. His record was intact. Like I told you, Tom was never late for work!

Discipline Learned (or Not) in the Cadet Corps

I met Frank, known to his teachers as Francis and to his buddies as "Chub", in my second year of high school. Frank was sixteen then and no longer in the cadet corps. The following tale might explain why.

At cadet summer camp in Ipperwash, Ont., two years before we had met, the cadet corps administrators had used various methods and assigned duties to instill discipline in the 14-year old Frank and others like him. One duty was bed making in which the heavy army blanket had to be pulled taut and folded underneath the mattress. The sergeant then came along on inspection and threw a quarter on the bed. If the quarter bounced up in the air, your bed passed inspection; if it didn't you had to pull all the bedding apart and start again. This routine was repeated until the quarter bounced when tossed on your bed!

Strict punishments for not following the rules were meted out regularly. Because Frank loved movies, sometimes he would sneak into the rec. hall and watch a movie when he was really supposed to be on duty. When he was caught for this demeanor (or for any other), his punishment was the cleaning of a part of the parade square. This doesn't sound too bad until you learn that he had to do it with a toothbrush! I think one session of this would have been enough for me, but Frank says he had to do this several times!

Another time he was in this same rec. hall watching a play and, unbeknown to him, a real donnybrook was taking place in his barracks. All the beds were upset except Frank's and one other cadet's. Frank had to return to the barracks when the play was interrupted by the announcement, "All those in Charlie Company get back to your barracks immediately." Because only the two beds remained intact, these two cadets (Frank being one) were assumed to have been the guilty ones and were assigned the task of righting the bunks and making all the beds. Once again, inspection with the bouncing quarter routine took place. But that wasn't punishment enough! Next morning Frank was summoned bright and early to clean the latrines and this continued for two days. On the third day he was assigned the sweeping of the barracks. "Rebel Frank" swept the dirt under the bunks and soon found himself back cleaning latrines!

Sunday was the day for airing grievances. Frank explained to the Captain that this was *the end* for him. He was sick of cleaning latrines as punishment for something he had not done, and he was going home. The captain said, "Oh, you can't do that."

"Watch me!" retorted Frank. That night he quietly climbed out the window, up and over the fence, and hitchhiked home, arriving at the Campbell farm sometime in the middle of Monday night. Times were tough and going A.W.O.L. meant you didn't get paid, so Frank's Mom put him on the bus that very next morning. By Tuesday night he was back in Ipperwash to face the music.

That September after high school had resumed, the Cadet Corps Major told Frank that, because of the poor record he had earned at Ipperwash, he would be stripped of his lance corporal stripe. Having had enough of rules and regulations, Frank told him that rather than ruin the uniform, he'd give them the whole uniform, stripe and all. Immediately Frank was given the choice of demotion or detention! Frank chose detention. For that entire year he went to the detention room rather than the cadet training sessions.

It would seem that some people are just not army material!

Murphy's Law

My friend, Yvonne, was soon to be a mother-of –the- bride. Daughter Alison was getting married. In talking with her friend Rene, Yvonne mentioned that she must start thinking about shopping for a dress for the wedding.

"Oh, don't do that," Rene said. " I have so many dressy dresses that I've worn only once or twice. Come to my house some day soon and I'll find you something. I'm sure you'd fit into any of my dresses, no problem."

"Oh no, I couldn't think of imposing like that. It's really kind of you, but I'll just keep watching at the malls and there'll surely be something I'll like."

"But, Yvonne. They're so much money. That's crazy. You come on Friday afternoon this week. I have no other commitments and we'll just see what we can come up with from my closet. If nothing suits, then you can try the malls."

Yvonne could see that Rene was sincere and so she finally agreed.

Friday afternoon saw her admiring Rene's many fancy dresses. Not only did she offer dresses, but also a purse, shoes and jewellery to match each one.

"You could open your own shop," Yvonne chuckled as she slipped into a peach-coloured suit. After trying on four or five others, she finally decided on a blue-beaded two-piece outfit and was so grateful to have her shopping finished and to have had the help of such a good friend.

Days later she modeled the outfit for a couple of other friends who assured her that, although it was different than her general choice of clothes, it suited her well and she definitely looked like the mother-of-the-bride.

About three weeks before the wedding, Allison and Paul were home for a visit. Yvonne was anxious to get their approval of her outfit. She quickly slipped into her new apparel and then strode into the living room where the family was waiting for her arrival.

Paul and Allison looked at her in astonishment. Then they

looked at each other with a definite look of disbelief. Paul stifled a chuckle and Allison sent him a warning look.

"What's the matter? Does it really look that bad?" Yvonne asked, just a little shaken by their reaction.

"Well…" Allison began, searching for the right words.

"What's wrong? Really! Tell me!"

Yvonne checked herself in the mirror but couldn't see anything amiss.

"Mom, you won't believe this," Allison said, shaking her head, " but Paul's mother is planning to wear the same dress and in the very same colour!"

Paul could not control his laughter any longer. "You two will look like the Bobbsey twins. Do you suppose it will start a trend?"

At this point Yvonne collapsed in hysterics, just picturing the whole thing, especially the family wedding photos. When she finally gained control she assured them that she would look for something else. "Really," she said, "I had misgivings about wearing someone else's clothes anyway. What if I spilled something on the dress or somehow ripped it? I'll feel better having my own, although I must admit I'll never get one this cheap!"

Well, Murphy's law being what it is, Yvonne did buy a different dress, but, unknown to her, so did Paul's mother. Neither of them wore the beaded blue dress! Luckily, this time they had not chosen the same dress!

The ABM Ate It

In 1986 I was very timid about using either a credit card or a debit card (I shudder thinking how many pieces of plastic line my wallet now). In fact, I had only one debit card, a Sears card, and a MasterCard. Remembering my pin number for that debit card and what procedure to follow at the bank machine was a real challenge. My college-student son would help me if there were no spectators, but most of the time he pretended he didn't know this technically-challenged middle-aged woman (translated "dinosaur"). Most of the time I went inside and stood in line waiting for a teller, along with the seniors. Only in an emergency did I face the "green machine". Of course, that happened only once in a long while and didn't give me the repetition I needed of using the machine and my pin number so that I could become "machine-friendly".

One day after work and a hectic round of shopping, I realized that I was too late for the banks and I was low on money. The weekend was approaching. I'd better have some cash. So I summoned up my courage and approached the box on the wall. I gingerly inserted my card in the correct slot and waited for the directions that would tell me to type in my secret pin. I listened to the whirring and grinding sounds, each second expecting the usual command. Several people had lined up behind me, waiting their turn. The machine noises stopped finally and the screen lit up. In disbelief I read the words "Out of Order". I groaned, as did others behind me. I pushed the button to retrieve my card. Nothing happened. I did it again. Same result. I was now questioning whether I was the one at fault but wanted to save face. I thanked the man behind me who suggested I bang on the bank window because there were still employees there and told him that maybe I'd go and phone them.

As soon as I was away from that line of people who now could get no money, I checked my wallet. Sure enough, there sat my debit card. What was missing was my MasterCard. I had single-handedly crippled the machine, probably for the whole weekend, by sticking in the wrong card! Now my dilemma was, how could I retrieve my card?

I furtively slinked away hoping no one would realize what had caused the machine to become "out-of-order". Driving home I was contemplating what to do. I knew one of the tellers rather well and I had to pass her house to get home. Maybe she could advise me.

Scarlet with embarrassment, I explained to her what I had done. If she had scolded me, I would have felt I deserved it. "The customer is always right" just didn't seem to fit this situation! Fortunately for me, she was very tactful, called the manager and arranged for the card to be retrieved and held at the bank for me until Monday.

" Normally it would be sent to head office," she explained.

"Other people have done this?" I asked.

"Now and then it happens," she smiled.

Back in the car I realized that I had never asked whether or not the machine would be operating as soon as my card was rescued. I sure hoped so. At that time this was one mistake I prayed I would never have to admit to anyone, especially my son.

You Know You're Having a Bad Day When...

My husband works in civil engineering and is sent to supervise different road construction jobs. Often this involves staying at a motel overnight. Usually it's pretty routine. Check in, watch T.V., fall asleep with the alarm set for 5:30 A.M., dress and go for breakfast.

One day last week this routine was somewhat interrupted about 6 A.M. It was raining with violent winds sending the spray everywhere, and it was cold, not your typical October day. Frank was more than ready for a java jolt. Suitcase in one hand and his laptop computer in the other, he hurried against the gale to his parked car. The jolt he received there certainly awakened him! No need for coffee, except maybe to steady his nerves. Both front side windows of his Volkswagen had been smashed in, the interior was soaked, and glass littered everything! A quick survey told him that his cell phone, cheque book and bankcard, and a few receipts were gone. The adrenaline was pumping. Back he hurried to the motel to get the desk clerk to dial the police! She didn't speak English, didn't know "police". Another adrenaline rush! Frank took over, called the police, and paced until they arrived.

Finally the details were recorded, and Frank threw some newspapers on the driver's seat and headed for the job site. He had a crew there waiting for his advice. Pulling in to the M.T.O. yard, he decided he'd better park in the oversized garage and try to keep any more rain from getting into those gaping windows.

He supposes he was the best part of an hour getting construction details worked out and questions answered. Finally he headed back to the car, by now convinced that the worst was behind him. The site that met his eyes was unbelievable. His lonely little open-aired Volkswagen was bedecked with more pigeon poop than he had ever seen in one place. It was as if one hundred and fifty of them had had target practice! The car wash was out of the question unless he wanted to be washed inside and out. I guess it's times like this that you really know the meaning of "being shit upon"!

The "Origin" of Mother's Day, According to Frank

Years ago Frank was asked by the minister to take his turn the following Sunday to tell the children a story. It was Mother's Day and Frank had hoped to find something worthwhile to tell about the day's origin. The encyclopedia offered little (this was before the days of internet) and so, with a lighthearted approach, he devised the following story. I am including it in this book because of the many friends who have requested it!

A long time ago when cities were a lot smaller than they are now, and more and more of the people lived on small farms in the country, things moved at a lot slower pace than they do now.

The people, though, were not without problems. One of the difficulties they had was that the barn areas of the farm were infested with mice. The mice would get into the grain areas of the barn and destroy the seed grain for the following year.

To solve this problem, the men got together at one farm and taught the cats how to catch mice. Ever after that when the farmers travelled around to visit one another, they noticed that some of the farms had fewer mice than others. Whenever an enquiry was made about this fact the farmer would say, "That old cat is a great mouser."

Besides the problem in the barns, people also encountered a different problem in their houses. Most of the clothes and all of the blankets were made of wool from the sheep on the farm. Moths would get into the clothes closets that usually had only a curtain hanging over the front, and would chew great holes in everything.

The men got together once again and taught the women how to catch moths and how to mend the holes in the clothing and blankets. This created a problem because the women were so busy that the men had to do the cooking and look after the children along with all the other work on the farm.

The families were so appreciative of what the men were doing that they would get together, usually on a Sunday in June, and have a special day for the fathers, but I am getting off the track here and that is another story.

When the men sat around in the evenings, they would brag about what good *"moth*ers" their wives were, but this did not solve the problem of all the work the men had to do. "If we could just think of some way to reduce the number of moths," they would say. Then one evening they came up with the idea of camphor and mothballs.

These inventions reduced the number of moths so much that, over a period of time, there would only be a few localized outbreaks at the beginning of the moth season, usually around the first week of May. The women would take some little thing from the cupboard, like olives, cheese, and mushrooms, and they would gather wherever the moths were and catch them all. Afterwards they would bake a pie and have a party while the men were at home tending to the work. They named the day *"Moth*ers Day".

As the material for clothing and bedding changed, there were fewer and fewer moths around but the women had gotten so used to getting together that they carried on the tradition. On the first Sunday in May they would take the unusual ingredients, bake the pies, and have a party.

One year, the lady where the "*moth*ers" always gathered got thinking that the pies they made tasted so good that maybe she could sell them all year. Well, everyone agreed that was a good idea.

When this lady went to open her new business she did not think that *"Moth*ers" would be a good name so she changed it to "Mothers' Pizzeria" and had a special every *"Moth*er's Day".

And that, my friends, is my version of the origin of Mother's Day!

Also by Heather Campbell

The Show Must Go On is a mixture of history and entertaining tales, telling of rural life and the entrepreneurial spirit of the author's parents, Howard and Hazel Gunter, of Coe Hill, Ontario. If you lived in the 1920 to 1970 era, you will identify with so many of the experiences. If you are younger, you will appreciate the timeless humour, moral struggles and human foibles. This is a little treasure chest of a Canadian family's history, as well as stories of the author's early years.

ISBN 155395794-6   Trafford Publishing $19.85
www.trafford.com

ISBN 141203302-0